Thirteen Roses

Book Four - Alone

Michael Cairns

Cairns Publishing

Amersham, Buckinghamshire

Cairns Publishing
Hollywood, Weedon Hill, Hyde Heath
Amersham, Bucks HP6 5RH
www.cairnswrites.com

Publisher's Note: This is a work of fiction. Names, characters,
places, and incidents are a product of the author's imagination.
Locales and public names are sometimes used for atmospheric
purposes. Any resemblance to actual people, living or dead, or
to businesses, companies, events, institutions, or locales is
completely coincidental.

Book Layout & Design ©2015 - Michael Cairns with Book-
DesignTemplates.com

Thirteen Roses - Book Four - Alone/ Michael Cairns. -- 1st ed.
ISBN 978-1-909699-60-1

This one's for Rich

Foreword

I love writing about London. I love stories based in London, especially ones featuring zombies, of which there aren't nearly enough. I think the first two lines of this book are my favourites from the entire series, which possibly says a lot about my sense of humour, but also about my love of being English.

Part One

Krystal

The hospital was clean. Bayleigh said that was first time that could ever be said about an NHS hospital. Krystal hadn't spent enough time in them to know, but then, they weren't talking about that sort of cleanliness anyway. The hospital was clean because of the huge mound of zombie bodies outside the front and the silence that ran with her down every hallway.

She'd tried, last night, to explain to Bayleigh what it felt like being in here. It was like having her own home, one that no one could kick her out of. Ed felt it too. Less than her perhaps, because he still yearned for the home he hadn't been too long out of. But for her the new world was, in one way at least, a blessing.

Today was particularly exciting, because today she was going out with Luke. He was the only one who'd left the hospital in the four days since the cavern and she was antsy for the outside. He was taking her because they didn't know how much longer they had until the devices ran out and that meant the zombies would be coming. She needed experience in fighting and killing them. They all did, but Luke had decided she and Bayleigh stood the most to gain from a bit of practice.

Jackson had grumbled and moaned, but he'd seemed calmer in the last couple of days. His frustration at sharing a hospital with a hundred hot chicks and not getting laid gave Krystal endless amusement, and at least he hadn't talked about God recently. In fact, in a weird-off between him and Dave, Dave won every time.

He'd emerged from the cathedral an entirely different person, one none of them could understand. He'd spent the last four days strolling around the place, poking at things and playing with them, but showing no interest whatsoever in doing anything. He had to be reminded about how dangerous the zombies were every time he talked about going out for a stroll. It was like he'd been lobotomised. Once Bayleigh explained what that meant, Krystal had agreed.

She reached the top of the escalator and raced down it. They'd switched them off three days ago to save power. She didn't know how the electricity worked, but Alex was pretty certain they would only have it a month or so, assuming nothing went wrong. He said if a power station blew up then all bets were off.

She reached the front door and put her hands on her knees, panting and out of breath. Luke strolled from the reception area and smiled. 'You alright?'

'Yeah, just checking on things.' She replied.

'Things?'

'Windows, emergency exits, you know, the stuff you said I should check.'

'You know, that's another reason we're going out today. Four days of hiding in here and everyone's forgotten what the zombies are like.'

'I can't believe the hostages haven't even met any yet.'

'Sad but true. Perhaps we should introduce them in a safe environment before the devices stop working.'

'Is there such a thing as a safe environment any more?'

Luke shrugged and tossed her the sword. 'Shall we?'

She grinned and nodded as she strapped it on. It felt good hanging at her waist and she felt safer with it on. Not safe, but safer. How anyone could forget what the zombies were like was beyond her. She still woke every night, sweating about the boy in Canary Wharf clutching her wrist as he died, or the frantic car ride through the city to reach St Paul's. Sometimes she woke seeing Ed strolling down the front path like he was going for the morning paper. She wasn't ever going to forget the zombies.

Luke pressed the emergency button, the door hissed open, and they stepped outside. There were a few zombies with long memories waiting at the barrier, watching them with hungry eyes. Between them and the zombies, however, were two motor-bikes with helmets slung over the handlebars. She grabbed one and put it on, then slung her tiny leg over the bike.

It was small, made by Yamaha, and, according to Luke, almost as deadly at the zombies. Her feet just scraped the ground and she wobbled until she rocked to one side and put her foot flat on the floor. He'd explained how it worked a bunch of times and she'd ridden around the ground floor of the hospital, but doing it with an audience of zombies was an entirely different prospect.

She started it beneath Luke's watchful gaze and couldn't help grinning at the throbbing between her legs. This would never have happened in the old world. She used to watch them roll past down Embankment but never dreamed she'd ride one her-self. She let the clutch out, rolled forwards and glanced sideways at a zombie.

The bike stalled and juddered to a stop. She blushed, pleased for the helmet that hid her red-dening cheeks, and tried again. Luke was already astride his and rolled up beside her. 'Know where we're going?'

She nodded, focusing on the handlebars and the throttle. It was going to work this time. She rolled forwards and the bike chugged happily. Luke eased past her and slammed on the revs, heading for a gap in the zombie line.

He brushed between two of them, their reactions far too slow as they grabbed for him. She followed suit and laughter burst from her throat as she swept past them and onto the road. They were everywhere, but the fear was gone as they raced past in a blur. She fixed her eyes on Luke's back but soon realised she needed to do more. The moment Luke found a gap between the zombies it closed, and she had to find an alternative route.

She started to relax on the bike. Luke said he'd got one light enough for her and it was easier now she was going fast, but her arms were aching long before they reached the river. It reeked down here. There were more bodies on the ground, and piles of bones drying in the late autumn sunlight. The zombies were turning on one another.

Luke said they were forming into packs, the stronger ones finding those weak and alone and tearing them apart. They cruised past a park on the right of Embankment and what lay within nearly sent her careening into the wall. As many as twenty zombies hunched in a rough circle. In the centre she saw a mound of half-chewed corpses and bones.

They were organising. Luke said it was like going back ten thousand years to when man began learning, drawing together the first scraps of civilisation from chaos. They would move onto tools soon and then, as Jackson put it, they were fucked. Her eyes flicked back to the road and she shouted in alarm.

A zombie was right in front of her. She hauled on the handlebars and her heart lurched sideways as she realised she'd screwed up. The front of the bike turned but the back couldn't follow it. The rear wheel popped off the ground and threw her off. She slammed into the zombie followed closely by the bike.

Krystal landed helmet first, and flipped onto her back, breath charging from her lungs like it was trying to escape the zombie on its own. The zombie crunched as, by blind luck, the bike drove it into the tarmac. The sound of breaking bones and squishing flesh was replaced with a horrible scraping sound as the bike slid along the tarmac.

She rolled onto her side, dragging in air between gritted teeth. She was determined not to cry. If she showed any weakness at all, Luke would take her back to the hospital and replace her. That wasn't happening. The bike screeched to a halt.

The zombie was mashed, face broken open and brain spilling onto the road. She rose as fast as her bruised body would allow. The zombies were closing, three almost within reach.

Luke had prepared her for this. She knew the theory, but stepping slowly and calmly backwards was the hardest thing she'd ever done. Sweat ran down the sides of her face despite the cool air and she gripped her trousers in her sweaty palms. The first zombies went for the corpse, ignoring her, and her mouth fell open. It worked. She had seconds before the corpse was swamped and they came for her, but that was all she needed.

She limped to her bike, got her weight beneath her shoulders, and hauled it upright. She tried, and failed, to look in all directions at once. But she did notice Luke, circling her slowly, bike revving. Was he near enough to help if she wasn't quick enough? Maybe not, but then that was the point, wasn't it?

The growl alerted her to the zombie before she saw it, and she jumped. She clutched the bike and kept it up, then booted the kickstand. She let out a breath as the weight left her back, and turned to face the zombie. It was only metres away, reaching for her, and she squealed.

She hadn't been near one in almost a week and she'd forgotten how alien they looked. Its eyes were sunk so deep into its face as to be almost non-existent, dirty red holes in crumbling sockets. She'd remembered their skin looking waxy, but in the week since the plague began, it had changed. It looked more like the piles of old concrete workmen left lying around the city, craggy and white and crumbling in the sun.

Her sword came out of the scabbard before she thought about it. She flailed at the creature, wincing at how clumsy she suddenly felt. The blade bit into the zombie's arm but it lurched on, reaching with dirty claws. It bashed her helmet and whipped her head sideways. She grunted and stepped back, banging into her bike. It wobbled but stayed up and she cursed herself. Clumsy and slow and stupid.

She leapt sideways, away from the bike and the zombie. It swung slowly round towards her but she had the time to set her sword properly. It came again and she hacked at its hands. The left one came completely off and the other was left hanging by skin and tendon as blood glugged out in lumpy jets.

It wasn't bothered, so she stepped sideways and raised the sword, her confidence returning. She swung horizontally, aiming for the neck. The zombie lurched at the last moment and she got it in the jaw. The sword smashed its teeth in and cut straight through its cheek. It lodged for a moment in its face before she yanked it free.

The zombie swayed, still not exhibiting any signs of pain. It looked more confused by the gouts of blood and tongue streaming from its mouth. She stepped around it and another zombie crashed straight into her. She screamed as she tumbled to the ground, sword flying from her outstretched hand. She rolled over, covering her head. She didn't need to.

The zombie was already locked in an embrace with its wounded comrade. Its teeth were locked around its face, tongue lapping at the blood in a grotesque impersonation of a kiss. She froze, swallowing down the bile and wondering how much of it was remembered from before it died and how much was greed. Then she blinked. They weren't the only two zombies in the world, even if it felt like it to them.

She turned back to her bike, checking about as she reached for the handle bars. More were coming but their eyes were focused on the snogging, blood covered zombies and she climbed on without further mishap. The engine was still chugging away and she raised the kickstand and got going. She didn't stall and, thanking Luke's dad for the miracle, got up to speed.

Luke came along side. 'Not a bad effort. Not a good start, though. That could cost you.' He pulled closer, slowed and handed over her sword. She flushed, grateful again for her helmet, and took it from him. The bike wobbled as she stuffed it back in the scabbard.

She wasn't sure what he meant by the last bit, but he'd said not a bad effort, and she'd take that for starters. They raced side by side down the river, weaving this way and that. They passed a set of young zombies in yellow overalls. It was, she realised with an ache in her gut, a school trip. Kids her age bumbling aimlessly, searching for food. Were they a pack as well? Did they gather around the body of one less fortunate to feast on raw flesh?

She didn't want to think about it, but she had no choice. This was the world now and there was no escaping it. Luke had tried to explain it to them. He talked about what lay ahead. The food would go off pretty soon so they needed to find livestock and learn how to care for them. They had a hundred extra mouths to feed as well, so the trips to the supermarket had become a daily event for Luke. It was one reason for this mission.

The internet was still up. Alex had tracked down a distribution centre for Tesco so now they had to take a look and see what state it was in. That she was excited about visiting a warehouse was maybe a little sad, but she didn't care.

Luke had talked about other things too. They needed to find somewhere safe, somewhere more permanent than the hospital. Somewhere outside London. She shuddered at the thought, but he was right. There were places only a few hours away that would be empty of zombies. She imagined being able to stand outside without one hand on her sword hilt and grinned. That was worth leaving the city for.

Luke waved a hand as they crossed Westminster bridge and she slowed. She could see all the way down the river from here and if she half closed her eyes it looked as though the plague had never happened. Then she crested the bridge and she saw why Luke had slowed her. Coming towards her over the bridge was an army of zombies.

They wore black, for the most part, t-shirts bearing symbols from metal bands. Many of them had long hair that was coming out, grey lumps of scalp visible where their locks were missing. And they had glasses on, cardboard glasses with red and green lenses. Beyond them, the Imax Cinema rose into the morning light.

Jackson

He was suffocating. God hadn't meant for him to be in here, trapped with all this temptation. He groaned and rearranged his junk inside his pants, leaning back in the plastic chair. He hated the chairs, hated them. They were a curse upon humanity, a scourge only one level below the plague itself. And it did things to the ladies.

There were three of them in the room with him. He was idling, looking at stuff on the net, but his eyes kept leaving the screen of his phone. They were on the same crappy chairs and were as uncomfortable as him. So they fidgeted, pushing their butts forward and thrusting out their titties. He couldn't keep his eyes off them. And they knew it. They knew what they did to him.

He'd seen it again and again as he strolled around the place. They gave him looks, come-ons that fled when he went closer. They wore those jogging pants that clung to their legs and arse and they knew it. They all knew it. He growled and swallowed it before the ladies heard.

They were laughing at him.

He'd asked a couple of them. He'd made it clear who they'd have the honour of screwing but they hadn't been interested. They smirked and said sorry like they meant it but he knew better. He glanced down at his phone. He was bored. Bored of surfing the same sites that didn't change and didn't update. Bored of watching the same looped messages on all the TV channels. And he was bored of being in this damn hospital.

He shoved himself out of the chair, earning a look of surprise from the three bitches. They watched him leave the room and it took till he was out the door before he realised what he'd called them. He stopped, one hand against the wall, head hanging down.

He'd got complacent. He wasn't doing God's work anymore and he'd got lazy. He couldn't stand being here. That was what was wrong.

He shook his head and straightened, letting out a breath as he put his hands to his belt. He could blame everyone he wanted, it didn't make it any less of a sin. He strolled down the corridor, nodding to another of the ladies as he passed. She gave him the sort of smile that made him hard and think about grabbing her and taking her with him into his room.

Had she sinned? They'd all sinned, every last one of them. They were all playing this innocent thing but it was bullshit. And he would call it. If he was here any longer he would have to call it. The door to his room hung open. Nothing to hide and nothing to steal.

He entered, closed the door and removed his belt. He knelt. He wanted to pray but he didn't know how to anymore. Everything with Luke and the demon and the soldiers of God had left him in limbo. He was God's chosen, he knew that, but he didn't know who God was anymore. He didn't understand why God would let the plague happen. Sure, there were a lot of people the world was far better off without, but he was one of them. Or he had been.

So instead of praying, he counted, the belt sounding like a gunshot as it opened the skin on his back. He stopped when he reached seventeen and his arm went numb. The sin was there, lurking beneath the surface, but he'd driven it deep and it would stay there for a while. They were ladies, deserving of every respect he could give them. And anything else he could give them as well.

He grinned, stood, and collapsed face first onto the bed. The world spun and he moaned into his quilt. He would lie here for a minute. But then he was going out.

He wasn't sure how long he lay there, but when he stood, the wounds on his back split open and set his skin on fire. The pain reminded him of his sins and he bathed in it until it dimmed enough for him to move. He dressed, finding clean clothes on the chair. The ladies knew how to use a washing machine and he wasn't paying for clothes anymore. If it was up to him, he'd wear something new every day, but Bayleigh insisted.

He sniffed and shook his head as he left the room and stomped to the front door. His gun hung over his shoulder. He only had a few rounds left, but he didn't intend on using it. He had other methods. The reception device was hidden in one of the drawers at the front desk. All the survivors, the ladies and the original crew, were crammed into one small ward that was guarded by the other three devices. They wouldn't miss this one.

And if they did, so what? There was no law here, no one to tell him yes and no. He was God's messenger. Taking the device meant he could go out and hunt and that was something they should all be thanking him for.

He shoved the device deep into his pocket as he strolled through the front door. The zombies were restless this morning, probably pissed off at missing Luke and Krystal when they left on the bikes. She'd been so damn happy about it he could spit. Luke said Jackson didn't need the training and thought that would make him happy. He scowled. The little tit didn't get it. It wasn't about training, it was about using the right person for the job, and Luke had got it all wrong. But then, he got a lot of things wrong.

Jackson took two steps from the hospital before a voice stopped him.

'Where are you going?'

He pressed his lips together, took a deep breath, and turned. Dave stood just inside the doors. He was Dave now. He'd told them all in that weird-boy monotonous voice he'd started using and no one had wanted to argue. There was a lot about him Jackson could argue with, but he didn't. It would be like kicking a rabbit. Though that would probably be fun if you had something to kick it at.

Dave wasn't fun. Not in any way. Just talking to him made Jackson's skin crawl, and it took a lot to do that.

'Out.'

'What about the zombies?'

Jackson sighed. It was never simple. 'What about the sodding zombies? What about them?'

'They're going to eat you.'

A grin spread across Jackson's face and he spread his arms wide. 'But, Dave, didn't you hear? I'm the chosen one.'

He strolled out and the zombies parted before him, shoved back by the barrier. He roared with laughter as he spun around and looked back at the hospital. Dave's eyes were wide. Then they narrowed and he raced back behind the hospital desk. Dammit. He was creepy but he wasn't stupid.

'You stole the device. You shouldn't do that.'

'Why not?'

A frown flickered across Dave's face, as though he couldn't work out why it was bad. But it was gone when he opened his mouth. 'Because there are people in here who rely on it to keep them safe.'

'People not meaning you. I don't know what you are.' He muttered under his breath before raising his voice. 'The ward's still safe. You might wanna get back in there.'

He was halfway across the street and the zombies nearer the hospital crowded in, clamouring for the open, unprotected doors. Dave's eyes widened again and he vanished into the hospital. Jackson chuckled and looked about him. He'd been diving once, with tanks and everything, when he and Clarissa went to Greece. There had been a moment of panic when the water closed over his head and his breathing had sped up till he was gasping in and out of the mask. He knew he needed to slow down, but there had been something so alien about it, so utterly wrong. It had taken him a while.

This was the same. The zombies surrounded him, staring with hungry eyes and reaching with clawed hands. And his breaths were coming short and sharp. This time, though, he smiled as his breathing slowed and he sauntered away from the hospital, just another chosen one out for a stroll in the city.

He hadn't thought about where he was going, just about getting out. But he was out now and fancied somewhere nice. Soho was unlikely to be much fun anymore, and he was about to head to Regent's Park when a thought struck him. He set off in the opposite direction, towards the city and the yard. Pavan wouldn't have had time to do anything with his van, so it would still be there. And his keys were in his pocket.

It was easy to get around town now there weren't any bloody suits. The zombies made a path and he strode through. He tried to hit one, racing quickly towards them, but somehow they stayed clear, scrabbling back to get away from the device. He was in a bubble, safe from the world. He needed to hurt something, to begin God's work, but it was impossible with the device.

He reached the yard quickly and sighed in relief as he saw the van. It beeped as he thumbed the keys and he hauled open the back doors. Benches on both sides, restraints hanging down to the plastic bottom. Putting that in had been a sod, but after the first bleeder he'd had to. It was early on. Some little brat had realised what was happening and he hadn't had the straps by then. Stupid kid had thrown himself about so bad his nose broke and he sprayed blood over everything. Now the interior was all wipe-clean surfaces.

He turned away, eyes stinging. He wasn't sure what was worse; what he'd done or not being able to find the remorse he felt sure should be there. He knew it was evil and wrong, but it was a different person who did those things, and a long time ago. It wasn't him. God saved him from that person and he was as dead as the zombies growling around the edge of the yard.

He climbed in the front and tried the engine. She rumbled into life and he thumped the wheel. This was better. This was good. He stuck it in reverse and put his foot down. He managed to catch a zombie before it scrambled free of the device field and sent it flying, its head smashing open as it struck the wall. He watched in the wing mirror as its pals set on it and sank their teeth in.

They weren't paying attention to him anymore. He grinned, teeth showing. Of course. He pulled the device from his pocket and placed it on the front seat, then slipped from the cab. He strolled calmly over to the feast until he reached the edge of the field. He hesitated, then jogged back to the van and opened the rear doors. He leant in and loosened four of the restraints.

Back to the feast that was already almost finished. Of the guy he drove into, there was only a few chunks of meat left on his rib cage and legs. His face had been stripped bare and Jackson could swear another of the zombies was chewing pieces of his nose off the strip of fleshy skin it had hanging from its fist.

He swallowed and turned away. That was pretty gross. He stepped closer but received no response yet again. He had maybe a couple of seconds before the food ran out. Without waiting any longer, he stepped over the line and grabbed one of the zombies from behind. He locked his arms around its shoulders, leaving its arms sticking out helplessly to either side.

The reaction was instantaneous. The zombie growled and lashed out with its feet, striking another in the face. It twisted and writhed and struggled but he gripped it firmly. The other zombies clawed at it, but Jackson stepped back over the line, dragging his captive with him. Its reaction this time, was quite different.

It screamed like a really bad metal singer, all gravel and no tune. For a moment it thrashed uncontrollably. He almost lost it before it went completely limp and unmoving. It was easy for Jackson to drag it over the yellow stones and into the van. He could feel the zombies watching him, their eyes tracking his every movement. They were silent as well, as if they knew he was doing something different, something other than killing them.

He sat the zombie on the bench and attached the bindings around its legs and arms. It still wasn't reacting, eyes flat and staring. The device had killed any urge it had to fight or eat. It was amazing. And dull. With a growl, Jackson pulled the crowbar out from beneath the front seat and headed for the line.

He didn't get close enough for them to grab him before he swung. The bar went straight through the first one's face, shattering its teeth and spraying them across the yard where they blended into the dusty stone. It was set upon and he paced around the circle until he found more willing sacrifices. The next one he bashed in the top of the head and his bar sunk in deep and got stuck. He hauled the zombie into the zone and dumped the body on the ground, then busied himself wiggling the bar to and fro until it came free with a sound like duct tape being torn off skin.

It still wasn't enough. He wasn't fighting, he was executing and there was no release in that. The bodies were good. Two less zombies to fight. But he needed release. He ran around the circle until he found a space in the line and dashed through it. He could imagine the other guys watching him, swearing and shouting at him what the hell was he doing.

They wouldn't understand. They weren't driven. Yeah, they wanted to stay alive, but they weren't here for God. They weren't here to save the world, so how could they know his pain? How could they understand how much it hurt being shut up in that damned hospital? They couldn't, and by the time he returned, his frustration would be gone.

He thumbed the safety off his gun as the first zombie came for him. The bar shattered its kneecaps and it fell face first. He ran around and took long strides towards the van. Two more got in his way and he swung. His first blow went in via the temple and emerged from its ear, throwing brain fragments across the floor. His return blow brought the sharp part of the bar into the other creature's head. His swing was weaker and the crowbar stuck in the thing's skull and hauled it around.

It stumbled and lost its footing as it landed within the device field. It thrashed about on the floor, arms and legs going like pistons before it stopped and lay still. He extricated the bar and kicked the body. Interesting that it could still fit for a moment even after he'd speared its brain.

He tossed it out of the field. It struck the floor and was set upon in moments. This was better. He was sweating, feeling it. He stepped out, then back into the field, and watched them as they ran at him and stopped. This was much better. He grinned and showed them his back. He peered in the back of the van at his captive zombie. It wouldn't be any fun with the device in the van.

He climbed into the front and gunned the engine, then pulled out of the yard. He'd ditch the device back in the hospital. That'd make Luke happy and keep him off his back. Then he could come back to the van. These things didn't register pain, but he would change that.

Bayleigh

She wanted to dislike them. They were so entirely easy to hate. Perfect skin and hair, nice smiles and great bodies. Things she'd never have noticed in a million years before she was forced to live in a tiny space with a hundred of them. That wasn't true. She'd have noticed, but in the same way she noticed shoes and hair styles. Nice and all, but not worth thinking about. Now she couldn't help noticing.

Sophie had these little dimples when she smiled that made her look sweet and made Bayleigh's toes curl. It was like she knew she had them and used them at just the right time. But despite all that, she found herself liking them. Which was why she was here in the centre of the ward. The room was long and thin with desks and nurses' stations running down the middle. There were a few comfier chairs here, and enough space for them to get together and chat. As per usual, she was right in the middle.

Without exception, the girls were all twenty three or younger. They were, for the most part, virgins, and painfully, scarily religious. They all attended church group and made the church a large part of their lives. And almost to a woman, were refusing to believe what Bayleigh found herself saying over and over.

'It can't be true. Why would they lie to us?'

Bayleigh sighed and resisted the urge to put her head in her hands. 'Everything has sugar in it. They say 'no added sugar', but that just means they haven't ladled extra spoonfuls in. Everything's got sugar in.'

Sophie hissed and turned away, raising her hand as if to block the truth out. Sugar wasn't the only problem. Apparently, she couldn't believe there were homeless people in the city like Krystal, who wasn't being fed by her local church. She also refused, point-blank, to believe that porn could be bought over the counter in shops in Soho.

Sophie came from Kent. She'd attended a church meeting two weeks ago, the same as usual, and been introduced by her Vicar to a lovely man called Andre. Andre had come from a far larger church and wanted to speak to some of the younger members of the congregation about their lives out in the sticks. She'd been happy to talk to him and, at her Vicar's urging, been honest and open. She hadn't found it strange when he asked about her parent's health and history of heart disease. And she hadn't found it odd when he held her hand. Her Vicar often did that.

She couldn't remember anything after the meeting until she woke up in St Paul's. Her story was a carbon copy of the other womens', only the details changed. She was unusual because she'd taken the news of a demon and two angels being here on Earth considerably better than most of the others. It turned out the others weren't quite as literal in their translation of the bible.

Bayleigh had a sneaking suspicion the girls had been chosen more for their breeding suitability than their religious leanings. Not that it mattered now. But Sophie was just unbelievably nice and Bayleigh needed a bit of that. She kept catching herself at the window, staring at the zombies. She lost hours studying them as they lurched about in their unhurried way.

They were so apathetic, so... meaningless. She'd spent her whole life working every second, except for the rare evenings when dad was peaceful and she could slump on the sofa and watch TV. Now there was a whole world of people whose only aim in life was to do nothing except eat. Watching them was oddly restful, yet deeply frustrating.

She thought she might be going a little bit crazy. She woke up most nights, bathed in sweat and struggled to get back to sleep. She wasn't the only one. Ed was finding it tough and Krystal was fronting but it was obvious she was struggling too. The last four days of down time had forced everyone to realise that this was life now and things weren't changing.

She thought she was dealing with it well. Considering she had the extra worry of when the weird effects from the spell were going to wear off, she was doing bloody great. She'd only slept four hours last night and woke feeling great. It was early afternoon, she'd had one slice of bread, and wasn't the least bit hungry. Luke had tried to talk to her about the spell but she'd blown it off and found a way to change the subject. She felt amazing. The comedown had to come soon, but right now, she felt amazing. At least, she had until she'd started talking about the dietary habits of those crazy non-Christian types Sophie had such a hard time believing existed.

'So what now?'

Bayleigh blinked as her reverie was disturbed. 'Sorry, what?'

Sophie's forehead was marred by the tiniest lines as she frowned. Bayleigh could almost hear her thinking 'say pardon, not what,' but she hid her smile.

'What are we going to do now?'

'Good question. Luke's talking about finding somewhere outside London, somewhere remote so there's less zombies.'

'Well yes, that makes sense, but I didn't mean that. I mean about the soldiers. They did kidnap us, after all.'

'And kidnap's really the biggest crime they've committed.'

'That's a good point. They've killed most of the human race and we're just going to run away to the country.'

'What good will it do us going back in there? They've got guns. They don't have you guys so they can't do anything bad in that way. What else would we do?'

'They deserve justice.'

'Oh, of course. So I'll just call up the police and get them on that then.' She stopped short of adding that she couldn't because they were all dead. She wasn't entirely convinced Sophie really believed that yet. She wasn't the only one of the ladies who stayed away from the windows. She'd taken to calling them the ladies now, just because it was convenient, but it still made her nose wrinkle.

Sophie was blushing and Bayleigh shook her head. 'Sorry, didn't mean to be rude. I'm just as frustrated as you. Seriously, what do you think we should do?'

'Well, there are a hundred and seven of us, yes? And I only saw about forty soldiers in that big cave, so we outnumber them. Couldn't we go in there and do a citizen's arrest?'

Bayleigh snorted and bobbed her head. 'Sounds perfect. Let's go.'

Sophie was half out of her seat and clapping her hands together, before she realised Bayleigh was joking. She went redder and Bayleigh felt absurdly guilty. It was like shooting fish in a barrel, only one without any water in.

'I see. I'm sorry I suggested anything.'

'Sophie, I'm sorry, don't be pissed.' There was the frown again. 'To be honest, as long as they're leaving us alone, I'd rather not rock the boat. They can't really do anything and...'

She trailed off but couldn't ignore Sophie's pointed look. 'I don't know whether anyone's mentioned this, but there are places like St Paul's all over the world, you know, with hostages in. All of those girls will have been... you know.'

She really hoped Sophie would know and she could see by the further wrinkling of her perfect brow that she did. Not having to explain was a small mercy, but she'd take it.

'Oh. That's terrible.' She put a hand to her nose, eyes sparkling wet, and Bayleigh took her hand.

'Yeah, it is. It's evil, though I'd never have used that word before this week.'

Sophie shook her head and pressed her lips together. Finally she spoke. 'So we're the lucky ones?'

'Yeah, in a way.'

'Ahem.'

They looked up to see another of the ladies hovering nearby. She was really young, not much older than Krystal, but shaped very differently. She was one of those whose hips swung when she walked and whose breasts pushed against her t-shirt. They were all prettier than her, and she could handle that, but when they were more shapely as well, it was just too much.

She beckoned her over. 'Hey, it's fine. Sorry, I don't know your name yet?'

'I'm Harriet. Lovely to meet you.'

She shook hands like they were meeting over a nice cup of tea and a scone. She settled herself smoothly on another chair. She probably jogged and only ate celery. Bayleigh thought she could find something close to dislike for this one.

'I'm sorry to bother you.' - Was that a glare from Harriet at Sophie? - 'But there was something I wanted to ask. The gentleman who is leading you—'

'Not sure I'd say leading. He knows more than us, but we're working together for the most part.'

'But you know who I mean?'

'Yeah.'

'Who is he?'

'I'm sorry?' Sophie would be happier with that.

'Who is he? He's isn't normal, is he? I saw him run in the cavern, when he caught that girl. He isn't normal. I only ask because I heard someone say something about an angel and of course that isn't true, but the thing above the cathedral was definitely a demon. I've seen them in books.'

The hardest part was getting used to someone who looked so much older than Krystal yet sounded about ten years younger. She'd seen demons in books. That was good, then. Bayleigh smiled. 'If you're sure that was a demon, why can't Luke be an angel?'

'Because angels are beautiful, transcendent beings that remind us of our own mortality. He's good looking in a traditional sort of a way, but he's not beautiful.'

'So it's about looks then?'

'Not just beautiful outside. There's something inside him that isn't right as well. Oh no, I've said that wrong. Not something wrong, just, he isn't pure.'

Bayleigh chuckled and nodded. 'I'm with you on that. Although in a way he is, because he's got even less experience at being human than you.'

Both of the ladies wrinkled their perfect brows and she nodded. 'Yeah, he's an angel. Only the Father made him human when he sent him to Earth. In our terms, he's about four weeks old.'

'I'm sorry, but who's the Father?'

'Oh, you know, god. Only, with a small g.'

Harriet looked like she was about to keel over. She nodded a few times, stopped and then nodded some more.

'I'm not going to become distracted by what is clearly a lack of understanding on your part. No offence. We have different beliefs, clearly—'

'Clearly.'

'Yes. So if Luke was an angel, which one was he?'

'He still is, just not physically. Well, not completely. And I think you'll have heard of him. What name does Luke sound a bit like?'

They both shook their heads and she sighed. 'He's Lucifer. I think people called him Morningstar as well, which is a pretty cool name, let's be honest.'

Harriet went white. 'The Deceiver.'

'That one's not quite so cool.'

The lady stood and stepped back, her chair scraping as it slid over the lino floor. 'I knew it. I said I could feel it.'

Her eyes left Bayleigh's and she looked across the room, nodding frantically. Bayleigh craned her neck and saw a group of ten or twelve ladies gathered by the door. At Harriet's nodding, they slipped out of the room. Bayleigh turned to talk to her but she was already racing after them.

'That was weird.'

Sophie nodded absent-mindedly. 'Is he really Lucifer?'

'He is, though he's changed.'

'Changed?'

'Yeah, he's nice now. Well, not nice, but not evil either. I don't know, I don't remember much about the bible.'

Sophie cleared her throat and Bayleigh realised she was about to get the full story. Then she realised she didn't want to know. She knew Luke. What she knew about Lucifer could fit on the back of a postage stamp, the words Bad Guy taking up most of the space. But Luke wasn't, at least not to her. How would it help her now knowing the evil stuff he'd done before?

She spoke before Sophie got the chance. 'What's going on with them?'

'I'm not sure. Why?'

'It just all looked a bit secretive. I'm not sure it's a good thing.'

'I'm sure it's nothing to worry about.'

'Sophie, I worry about everything these days.'

Alex

He couldn't stop staring. He knew he was staring and he still couldn't stop himself. She was amazing. She was beautiful in a way that made Bayleigh fade into the background. She made everyone fade into the background. He tried to tell himself it was her beautiful face. The way her nose sloped up just a little at the end and the full lips that curved up at the edges even when she was looking serious. Which was often.

But it was her tits as well. They were amazing and she kept wearing t shirts that were a little too small. He couldn't decide whether it was deliberate or just unlucky. Or lucky of course, depending on where you sat. He was sat in what had become the dining room and he was feeling pretty bloody lucky.

She looked angry and she was still gorgeous. She was called Harriet and came from Cambridge by way of West Thames University. She'd been living in Ealing while she studied and had some of the swagger of the girls from that side. He liked Ealing. If he'd known Harriet was living there, he'd have spent a lot more time there.

She smiled a lot when they spoke to one another. He wasn't superman when it came to girls but he knew the signs. And she hadn't been put off when he said he was a scientist. He didn't think she had much respect for what he did, but he had none whatsoever for her weird, blinkered religious views, so that was alright. And it wasn't like he was looking to build a long term relationship.

He knew he wasn't the only one in the place that was craving it. He'd seen Jackson prowling, making eyes at the ladies. He thought it made him desirable but it was borderline stalker and all creepy. Alex grinned and shook his head. The guy was a total nut job. At least the zombies gave him somewhere to direct his madness.

Harriet was going on and on to a group of the ladies about something, waving her arms around and looking heated. Every time she raised her arms, her t-shirt moved around and showed her tits off. Alex shifted in his chair and groaned in the back of his throat. The hospital was clean, there definitely weren't many zombies here, but sneaking off to a different part to masturbate was still a perilous task.

The ladies dispersed, heading out of the room. For a moment Harriet was alone and Alex strode over, trying to look casual while getting there before she had the chance to leave.

'Hey, how you doing?'

Her normal smile was absent when she made eye contact. 'Do you know who it is you're following?'

'Pardon?'

'Luke. Do you know who he is?'

'Of course.'

Harriet turned her nose up and looked past him.

'Why, what's the big deal?'

'He's the Betrayer. He's evil.'

'That's a bit strong, don't you think? He made a few mistakes, but he's atoned for them.'

'You can never atone for what he did.'

'Hang on. He spent thousands of years presiding over Hell. From the sounds of it, not much fun.'

'He could spend the rest of his life there, he would still never atone.'

'What happened to forgiveness?'

She jumped as though he'd poked her.

'I mean, just a thought, but you guys are all about forgiveness, right?'

'Us guys?'

'Christians. I mean, that's your main definer.'

'I suppose so. I'm also a student—'

'Were.'

'I was a student and a woman. They define me as much as my religion.'

'But not more. Look, the point is, aren't Christians supposed to forgive?'

'But what he did—'

'He did thousands of years ago. The Father's forgiven him, so—'

'Don't give me that. Who's this Father you all keep talking about?'

'God, whatever.'

She looked liked he'd slapped her. He only just restrained his smile. Her chest was heaving and he couldn't keep his eyes off it.

'It's not 'God, whatever'. It is God and I would thank you to be respectful towards my beliefs.'

'Hey, I'm respectful. But I've met the guy you call god and he doesn't like the name. That's all I'm saying.'

'Could you manage to talk to me without staring at my breasts for one minute?'

His face heated up and he glanced at the ground. 'Sorry. They are rather fine.'

She blushed bright red and folded her arms over them. 'That's neither here nor there. It's not polite to stare.'

'Yeah, sorry. Look, I don't want to argue. I came over to chat, not get in a fight.'

'You didn't do very well at that, did you?'

He grinned sheepishly and shook his head. She smiled back and unfolded her arms. 'Do you really like them?'

He burst out laughing and nodded. 'I like all of you.'

'Well that's lucky, you don't just get the breasts on their own, you know.'

'So what do I get?'

She blushed and frowned, glancing behind her. 'Nothing right now. Sorry, I have to go.'

'Wait, hold on.' She was already out of the room as he hurried to catch up. 'Where are you going?' It was a ludicrous question. There was nowhere to go. 'Can I come with you?'

She glanced sideways and shrugged. 'I suppose so.'

They hurried down the corridor, Alex doing everything he could to not stare at her breasts. He was in, unless he did something really stupid. His breath came in short bursts and he liked to think it was because of the stomping but he thought it might also have something to do with the way she moved in her jogging trousers and the thought he would soon get to see what lay beneath them.

They left the ward and raced down the corridor to the landing that filled the centre of the hospital. From here they went down the escalators to the front doors. The place was empty and Harriet hissed and tapped her wrist like she was wearing a watch.

'Expecting a visitor?'

She gave him a look and turned a full circle before finishing looking at him.

'Look, there's no one here. Why don't we go and hang out so—'

'Keep it in your trousers. They'll be here, we just have to be patient.' She paused, brow creasing. 'You might not want to be here.'

'Why not?'

'We're discussing things you might not want to hear.'

'I think I can handle it.'

'Your choice.'

She turned away and he put his hand on her arm, turning her back. 'So what were you studying?'

She looked around again before she let out a long breath and relaxed, leaning against the reception desk. 'I was doing a course in social work. Five years, so a long time, but lots of work experience, which was good.'

'So you've been out into the real world?'

She gave him another look and he raised his hands in defence. 'Hey, I only ask because I've spectacularly failed to do it. I went from school to uni and from there straight to the lab. I mean, I'm still at uni but I spent more time at the lab that anywhere else.'

'So what were you working on?'

'Oh, um, cures for germ warfare. You know, the modern chemical attack.'

'Oh wow, that's a really great thing to be doing. What could you cure?'

'Well that's just it. It's a tough field. We've got stuff that can help a lot, but nothing that nullifies the effects. That's still a way off. Longer now...' He trailed off, hoping he was looking suitably sad. There were less than two hundred people alive in England and he'd just lied to one of them. He thought he should probably feel worse than he did, but she was leaning in a way that made her trousers cling to her legs and show off this amazing profile. And she kept fiddling with this strand of hair that curled under her ear.

'So, have you done much work experience?'

She nodded. 'Yeah, some. I've just started my second year, but we shadowed a few social workers in the first year, so I've seen a bit. Enough to know Ealing isn't as glamourous as everyone says.'

'It really isn't. I've heard they've even got zombies living there now.'

Her laughter was cut off as he swore and shoved her behind him. Two zombies were strolling straight in through the front door. Alex only noticed from the swishing sound as the door opened.

'Shit, how the hell did they get in here? The devices must have run out.'

He grabbed her by the shoulders. 'Get up to the ward and find Bayleigh' - He ignored the look of disdain she gave him - 'tell her the devices have run out. She'll get everyone moving.'

Harriet stared at him with frightened eyes, frozen.

'GO!' She jumped and raced around him. He watched her arse for a moment before shaking himself. The zombies were closer and he ducked behind the reception desk. They'd spotted him so there was no getting away but they'd stashed a weapon here and that gave him a chance.

What the hell was he doing? This was unbelievably stupid, in every way possible, this was stupid.

He stood, shaking hands wrapped around the metal pole. He pulled open the drawer to get the device and stared at the empty space. Someone had taken it. The soldiers. It had to be the soldiers. They'd come in and stolen it. Had they taken the others? Krystal had been checking all the doors and she was diligent. This was the only way in.

His heart was trying very hard to get out of his chest and run away. His legs wanted to do the same thing but he kept them still. What if Harriet had stayed to watch? Instead they shook, so hard he expected to topple over at any moment. The first zombie reached for him and the world stopped. He saw its red eyes, horribly close and greedy, and he shouted and leapt backwards, flailing about him with the pole.

He succeeded in hitting precisely nothing, but got far enough away from the zombie to raise the pole in both hands between them. He just had to imagine it was a cricket bat or a golf club or something. He couldn't play golf. He couldn't play cricket either but he knew how to swing a bat. He swung as hard as he could, trying not to scrunch his eyes closed.

The tip of the pole struck the zombie in the back of the head with a sound like a cabbage hitting the ground. It sunk deep into its skull and stuck there. The zombie stiffened and collapsed to the ground and Alex gripped the pole with whitening knuckles. It tore free of the skull and he stared at the tip, and the blood and pieces of bone fragment stuck to it with rotting brain. The smell reached his nostrils and he couldn't believe he'd managed to forget it already.

He gagged and backed away, covering his mouth with his free hand. The other zombie fell to its knees and attached its mouth to the split skull. A sound like a misfiring vacuum cleaner filled the reception. Alex staggered towards the stairs, swallowing down the bile in his throat. He was about to climb up them when another zombie came in the front door, followed rapidly by a second. They would be free to roam in here. He couldn't let them get past and up to the ladies.

He took his foot off the steps and turned, raising the pole before him. He could do this. He had to do it. He imagined Harriet giving him that smile as she pulled her t-shirt off. That helped. Both newcomers joined their fellow eating the downed one, but the next through the door decided he looked tastier and rushed towards him.

Alex took a deep breath, then had it knocked out of him. Something slammed into his back, something that breathed hot and fast, and he shouted in alarm as the floor rushed up to meet his face.

Dave

Things were simple now. He couldn't remember a time when they weren't. He couldn't remember much of anything. Except the hospital. He knew how many steps there were and the numbers of every room and which corridors went where. He also knew how many index cards there were in the confidential records of over five hundred patients.

He was bored.

There wasn't anything to do and discovering that losing most of his memories left his brain wide open for other things wasn't much by way of a consolation. Although, knowing the hospital was fun. He thought it was fun. He couldn't rightly explain what fun meant, but he thought if he did know, then it would be.

He knew the names of every lady. They were nice, as far as that went. He wanted to fuck them. All of them preferably, but any would do. He didn't know why he wanted to have sex with them, it just seemed the right thing to do. He wasn't sure what right and wrong meant anymore either. It was all about where you were standing at the time. Although, he had come to realise, he wasn't standing anywhere.

Everything he saw came to him free of filters or prisms. He saw what happened and that was it. There was no judgment of it, so it meant nothing and couldn't be wrong or right. It just was.

There was one memory, though, since the change, that kept bobbing back up to the surface. He remembered the soldier he'd bumped into when he left the demon's lair. He remembered him so vividly, the look of amazement and the way his hands tightened around his gun. What was odd was that he remembered nothing after that. He remembered coming out of the church and nipping around the back of it to get close to Luke. But what happened in between was a mystery.

It didn't bug him, because he didn't really understand what it meant to be bugged, but he did recognise that it was odd. And it made him walk around, as though by using his whole body he could exorcise it and no longer be bothered by it.

He strolled now, down corridors that echoed the sound of his footsteps back to him, reminding him how alone they were. It was nice to be alone. He liked the silence. Something about that thought that made him wince. He'd been alone before. He shook his head. He couldn't remember it but it was there.

His ears pricked up. Someone shouted. They'd said 'Go', which didn't sound like something you wanted to hear these days. He picked up his pace, enjoying the clicks bouncing back and forth off the walls. There was a pattern to them, so he slowed and sped up, mind racing as he followed the different combinations.

Then he heard the thud that could only be something hard striking flesh, and everything changed.

He tried to hold on this time, to retain some part of himself as the mist fell, and he was successful. Partially. He was aware, but he had no control. He was only dimly aware of reaching the stairs and taking them four at a time. His balance was completely off and he started to totter. Somehow his feet caught up and he rushed down the stairs in a controlled fall.

There was someone at the bottom but he brushed past him, barely feeling the impact as he reached for the first zombie. Dave was moving fast and took the creature straight off its feet. They tumbled to the ground together, and with his teeth gritted hard enough to hear the grinding over the zombie's frantic growling, he shoved his thumbs into its eye sockets.

He remembered this, but the eyes he'd squashed before had been firm. These were like fruit after it had gone off, soft and yielding. The heat was the most surprising thing. It was like plunging his thumbs into a bolognese sauce as it simmered on the hob. He went through the eyes and his thumbs sank into something else, something almost as hot.

The zombie stopped moving and Dave growled and shook the head around by the sockets. He yanked it, gave it a twist, and felt something give. He knelt, heaving at the head until the neck ripped. With a howl of celebration, he tore the head off the body and raised it high. The zombie staggering towards him fell to its knees, and from his position hiding way back in his brain, he thought for one moment it was going to bow to him.

It did bow, until its mouth settled over the neck stem of its fallen comrade, and slurped at the blood streaming out onto the floor. He grabbed the top of its head by the scraggly hair still clinging to its pink scalp, lifted it, then slammed it down to the floor. The zombie growled and struggled, but only for as long as it took to get its teeth back into the blood. Dave did it again and again and the creature finally dragged itself away from its feast and sat up.

Its face was caved in, cheek bones flattened and nose pressed in. Nothing broken yet, though. With another howl, Dave rammed the head back into the floor and was gratified by the cracking sound. At that point, something pushed him from his precarious perch at the back of his brain and he spiralled down into darkness.

The floor was hard. And cold. His hands were warm. It was silent, save for his breathing. Someone else was breathing too, far harder than he was.

Where was he?

What had happened?

He scratched his face and his hand felt wet. He sniffed it and almost vomited. The stench of meat left out too long beneath a warm sun clung to his nostrils and climbed down into his gut.

He blinked but it remained dark. 'Where are we?'

'In a cupboard. Please be quiet.'

It sounded like Alex. Only he was terrified of something because his voice shook. 'Are they nearby?'

'I don't think so. I haven't heard anything for a while.'

'Oh.' What was he scared of? 'How did I get in here?'

'I dragged you.'

'What happened to me?'

'I hit you over the head with this pole. I'll do it again if I have to.'

'Oh. Why?'

'Why? You really can't figure that out?'

'Of course not. I heard you shout and came to help. Did you mistake me for a zombie?'

There was silence and Dave realised Alex was embarrassed. He didn't really understand embarrassment any more, but in this instance, he thought that perhaps Alex should feel it.

'It's okay, really. I understand. When zombies are attacking the first instinct is to hit anything that moves. I don't mind, really.'

'Dave, do you remember what you did to help me?'

What did he mean? 'I don't think I did help you.'

'You just killed three zombies with your bare hands. I hit you after the third because there weren't any left and I thought you were going to turn on me.'

'Turn on you?'

'Yeah, you know, throw yourself at me and rip my throat out.'

Dave thought about laughing. He didn't really know how to laugh but that sounded like something he would find funny. He tried it on for size and heard Alex gasp. The door cracked open and he saw Alex's face in the light that spilled through. He was pale and had the metal pole raised protectively.

'What's wrong?'

'You. God, what the hell is going on with you? One minute you've gone all weird and brain dead and the next you're a raving psycho.'

Dave shook his head. 'You aren't talking about me. I'm fixed.'

'Do you mean high? Because if you meant high, I'd agree. But fixed?' He shook his head. Dave was about to respond when Alex sneaked out into the corridor. He poked his head back inside. 'We need to get up to the ward. I need to make sure everyone's okay.'

Dave nodded. He needed to be near the action to make sure he didn't miss anything. Az was very interested in what happened here. He kept texting to see whether anything new had happened. Dave wondered if he was disappointed. He seemed disappointed when he responded that nothing had happened. Not that it mattered. He was doing his job very well indeed and that was what mattered.

They dashed down the corridor and up a flight of stairs, than back in the opposite direction. They didn't see any zombies and the ladies were still in the rooms. A larger group were gathered together in the lounge area, sitting on the tables and talking in low voices. Dave watched Alex stroll over, metal bar close to the floor.

He spoke to one of the women. Dave thought she was very beautiful. Her features were symmetrical and in good proportions. Beyond that, he didn't have a clue. He had, once. He had the vaguest sense he'd once have been in heaven being in this room. Now, though, it was just another room.

Alex came back, frowning and staring at the pole gripped tight in his right hand.

'Everything alright?'

Alex glanced up at him and then back at the pole. 'Not sure. I don't think it is. Where's Bayleigh?'

'I don't know.'

'Let's find her, shall we?'

Alex walked straight past him without another word and out into the ward. Dave was about to follow when he glanced at the gathering of ladies. They were staring at him and the way their eyes glittered beneath the lights reminded him of something from before his change. He thought it was snakes, or maybe some other animals, gathered around prey. It would have been chilling, had there been any logical reason for it. Instead it was just interesting. Lots of things were interesting these days.

He jogged after Alex, catching him as he went into the room they had unofficially dubbed the private area for anyone not a lady. Ed spent a lot of time in here, reading the magazines and books they'd scrounged off bedside tables when they were cleaning the place out. Right now, both he and Bayleigh were in there, Ed buried in a book and Bayleigh staring out of the wide window.

'Bay, I think we've got a problem.'

Dave blinked. He'd spent most of the last four days strolling the corridors, counting things. He hadn't heard Alex use that name for her. It was... surprising. Possibly. Bayleigh turned away from the window and nodded. 'Yeah, me too. Harriet, right?'

Alex blushed and Dave flicked his gaze back to Bayleigh. She was staring straight at Alex and maybe her cheeks were a little redder. He wasn't sure.

Alex nodded. 'That and more. Someone's taken the device by the front door. I just, well, Dave and I just saw off four zombies but there'll be more.'

'Who's taken it?'

Alex shrugged. 'No idea. Soldiers, I assume. It's easy to do if you can find it.'

'We should have hidden it better.'

'Maybe. Doesn't matter now. The hospital won't be safe for much longer. I thought it had run out to start with. That's going to happen soon.'

All four of them nodded. It had been a reoccurring theme since they got here. It was why Luke and Krystal were out today. They needed supplies for the road, and a way to travel.

'What about Harriet?'

'I just spoke to her. She's got the other girls in a flap about Luke. Apparently we're—'

'Being led by evil incarnate. Yeah, I had the same chat. She's a bit of a bitch, actually.'

Ed and Dave both started and stared at Bayleigh. She looked at them, eyebrows raised. 'What? She is. She knows she's hot and uses it to lead Alex around by the you-know-what and she's stirring up trouble. Luke saved her life and she's bitching about him. I can't think of a better word to describe her.'

That was a logical argument. Dave thought Bayleigh might be a bit jealous but he had no way of knowing. There was body language, some way of finding out what she really felt. He needed to do some research. That would be useful, to know what lay behind the words people spoke.

Alex opened and closed his mouth a few times, face red, before he found something to say. 'Anyone seen Jackson?'

They all shook their heads before Ed spoke. 'So what do we do?'

'About what?'

'Everything. What do we say to Harriet to stop her being a bitch and what do we do about the device?'

'I don't think there's anything we can do about the device. If it's gone, it's gone.' Alex said.

'Could maybe Harriet have taken it?'

Alex's face dropped at Ed's words, and Bayleigh nodded. 'She may well have. I don't know what she's planning, but if she thought she might be leaving, taking the device makes perfect sense. Do it now before anyone suspects you. Alex, was she with you at the front?'

Alex hesitated. 'Yeah, she was, but why would she go down there if she knew we might get attacked?'

Bayleigh thumped a fist into her other hand. 'It's the perfect cover, isn't it? Sneaky cow.'

Alex opened his mouth as if to argue, then shook his head. There was a lot of logic in what Bayleigh was saying, perhaps too much for Alex to defend against. Dave smiled and left them to it. They would find whatever conclusions they wanted and act on them. He needed to text Az. These were the most interesting things to happen all week.

He stomped away from the ward, finding a quiet corridor far enough away to be alone but near enough to still be inside the field made by the devices. He leant against the wall and started composing his text. He was halfway done when the sound of delicate footsteps distracted him.

One of the ladies made her way towards him. She was beautiful as well and very nicely put together. She had a blouse on and he couldn't help noticing the top couple of buttons were undone. By the way her breasts shifted beneath the material, he could tell she wasn't wearing a bra. He had the vaguest understanding that people who were strongly Christian should be chaste and modest, but that didn't always seem to be the case.

The lady swayed up to him and for a moment he thought she wasn't going to stop. When she did, her face was only a foot from his and he could feel her warm breath on his neck. He wondered for a brief second whether the plague had evolved into some covert strain. Then she spoke.

'Dave, right? I'm sorry, I had to find out your name. I'm Julia.' She stood on tiptoes so she could whisper in his ear. 'I want to suck your cock.'

He thought about explaining that the corridor was deserted so she didn't have to whisper, then her tongue flicked against his ear lobe and he realised this was all part of the act. The act implied she wanted something. He was tempted to play along. There was something familiar yet exciting about all this. He glanced down, straight down her top to her smooth pale skin, and his heart skipped.

He watched absently as his hand reached out and went around her waist, pulling her into him. She gasped at the sudden strength he used to haul them together. But she stayed where she was and her tongue grew more insistent, curling around the top of his ear. Something switched inside and his vision grew dim.

He could hear her breathing and every muscle in his body was suddenly tense. His hand grabbed her arse and squeezed hard. She stiffened a moment, then softened and wrapped her arm around him. The other went to the front of his trousers and rubbed. He growled into her neck as his vision turned red, then he lifted her and carried her until they came to a door.

Without looking to see whether there was anyone else in the corridor, without looking at anything at all, he kicked open the door of the room and took her inside. The red mist covered his vision and the world went away.

Luke

He almost laughed. They were faced by an army of movie-watching zombies. He squinted past them and saw a poster. The name of the film wasn't clear, but the word *Metallica* stood out. He'd heard of them. This rabble had been watching *Metallica* and now they were going to eat Krystal and him. Perfect.

Krystal gave him a look as they slowed at the top of the bridge. 'Shall we try the next one?'

He weaved back and forth, checking for gaps in the crowd. It was thick and showed no signs of breaking up. Something was driving them, keeping them together. Maybe it was the music, their love of metal forming some kind of unconscious bond. He laughed and shook his head. That was just daft. They were linked by the last thing they'd been doing, watching the movie.

It was an interesting thing to consider. Or it would be once they got through them and away. Krystal was right, though. There was no clear way through and there was no reason to risk it. He gunned the engine and got closer but they were packed in together. With a shake of his head, Luke swung the bike around and headed back towards Krystal.

She'd stopped, forgetting the first rule he'd taught her and already there were two zombies coming at her from behind. He pointed and she jumped, checking over her shoulder before hastily getting her bike moving. She was in time, though only just, and turned as he came past her. They raced together back to Embankment and around the front of the Houses of Parliament.

He glanced at the huge building as they rode past. It was beautiful. And it was filled with zombies in suits. He wondered whether they were still in session, sitting in their silly chamber shouting, or growling at one another. He cracked a grin as they headed past and up to Lambeth Bridge.

It was considerably quieter as they powered over the river. Krystal looked comfortable on the bike, just as she looked comfortable with the sword in her hand. She was wobbly in execution, but that would come soon enough. Between her, Bayleigh and Jackson, they had a half-decent chance of dealing with any zombies that attacked them on the journey out of town.

He hadn't discussed the entire plan with them yet. It meant more discourse and he couldn't be doing with that. He knew what they needed to do and the endless discussion was tiresome. He was hoping the ladies would agree with him and the others would just be carried along.

On the other side of the river they picked up the A2 and opened the throttles. The cars were piled thickly all the way down, crash after crash. This was something he still hadn't figured out abut their escape. Every major road out of London would be crammed, and getting a vehicle big enough to hold everyone would make it tough to get through.

On the bikes, it was a pleasure weaving through the cars. He lost himself in the movement, feeling how every lean transferred through the bike and into the wheels. He'd seen surfing and imagined it would feel like this, but never riding a bike. They never mentioned this sort of thing in the Flights.

He was so intent on the movement, he didn't see the zombie until way too late. It was leaning out of a car window, trapped but eager for freedom. The bike snapped off both arms and tore its head off, but the impact sent Luke flying.

He flew off the bike, over the bonnet of the next car along, and slammed into the rear window of the next. The gentle thud as an arm followed him over made his stomach turn as his head threatened to cave in. He heard the distant screech of tires as Krystal stopped, before the corners of his vision went dark.

He curled up on the floor, gripping his bruised skull, and lost himself in the hammering that made him want to vomit. Stupid, stupid, stupid. Five minutes ago he'd been criticising Krystal for not focusing and here he'd done exactly the same thing.

The pain lessened enough for him to sit up and be grateful there'd been no zombies near enough to take advantage. He blinked, looked around, and his heart jumped into his mouth like a stupid angel taking a swan dive off a motorbike. A zombie's face was pressed up against the window less than two feet from where he sat. Its lips were bared, exposed by cracked lips pulled back far enough for him to see the gums.

Its teeth clicked against the window and he shoved himself back until he bumped into the car behind. He sneered and rose to his feet, embarrassed at his most human emotion yet. He'd come here a month ago ready to cause havoc and now he was scampering from a zombie that couldn't even hurt him. He was weak and growing weaker every second.

A motorbike gunned next to his ear and he jumped again. Krystal was on her knees, hands tiny against the handlebars of the BMW he was riding. But the engine was ticking over. 'Thanks.'

'You alright?'

'I feel stupid, but yes, I'm okay. There's one you'll have to deal with before we get moving.'

He nodded past her and noticed the tight grin of anticipation on her face. He was also pleased to see her hand go straight to her sword. The zombie clambered over one of the cars towards the channel in which they both sat. Krystal stepped to meet it and as it put its hands on the bonnet, she hacked straight through both arms.

The creature fell straight forward, and ploughed face first into the car. He winced at the sound of its teeth shattering against the metal. It tumbled to the floor head first and Krystal buried the point of her sword in its head then yanked it out. She wiped the blade clean and sheathed it, then turned to him.

'What?' She asked.

He moderated his grin. 'Good job.'

She beamed. 'Thanks.'

She scampered back to her bike and mounted. He watched her for a moment, wondering why he felt pride. Why did he feel any of these things? She was nobody, one in billions... maybe that was it. She wasn't one in billions any more, not even one in millions. They'd done some rough calculations and figured the entire population of the Earth to be somewhere around a few thousand.

Of those, more than half were young, innocent women looking forward to a future of enforced child birth. The rest were soldiers or leaders of the soldiers, none of whom were people he'd trust to run anything, least of all Earth. So Krystal was, in many ways, the hope for the future. He chuckled and mounted his bike.

He followed Krystal back out onto the road and they sped down the A2. He kept his focus, despite the wind whipping his jacket and the beautiful lines he found between the cars.

There was a surprising lack of destruction on the ride. There were a few buildings where electrics had gone and fires started, but nothing had spread. Alex was confident there would be more destruction in time, as gas pipes eroded or backed up. There would be explosions and fires, neither of which would be good for zombies or humans. Getting out into the country was the only sane thing to do.

He laid on the gas and pushed past Krystal then guided her up a slip road. A petrol station sat at the top and he pulled in.

They'd planned this and Krystal went straight up to the shop. She parked her bike and scampered through the electric doors. She knelt and pressed the *lock open* button before heading for the desk. The clerk emerged from behind some racks, reaching for her, and Luke bit his tongue.

It was more difficult than he'd expected, watching in silence and unable to do anything. But she was already moving, dashing back around the aisle and drawing her sword from its sheath. She disappeared from view and the zombie lumbered around to the front door in pursuit. There was a flash of steel and the clerk's head, still wearing its cap, flew out of the open doors and bounced across the forecourt.

Moments later there was a clunk from the pump beside him as Krystal activated it. He stayed on his bike until she came out and stood near him, sword in both hands, rocking gently on the boles of her feet. She was a natural, just as he'd known. Where did his instincts come from? It could have been the millennia in hell, judging the sort of people who made attacking others a lifestyle choice. He certainly knew bad when he saw it.

He filled up the bike, rolled hers over, and did the same. Then they were back on the road, heading away from the main road and through a housing estate. The other side devolved into an industrial park watched over by the largest warehouse he'd ever seen. The car park ran along the back of the vast stone building where over thirty huge trucks were backed up to storage bays. He and Krystal drove around to the front and found an open door.

Luke squeezed in with his bike and Krystal followed. A small corridor led them back into a space large enough to fit a football field. Vast shelving units ran in rows all the way down the building, covered in shrink-wrapped pallets of food. He got back on his bike and they cruised down the first aisle.

Krystal opened her visor. 'It's like browsing at the largest supermarket in the world.'

'Only we have no idea what we're looking at.' In most cases, the food was obscured by the shrink wrap, identified by a tiny white label stuck to each pallet. They neared the end of the aisle and slowed. 'Do we need to open something and check its useful?' she asked.

Luke nodded, checked around him, and stopped the bike. He'd expected zombies, packers and whoever else would have been working here, but the place was deserted. He didn't believe that for a moment, but there were definitely none in the vicinity. He drew his sword and cut open the shrink wrap, exposing a wall of tins of baked beans.

Krystal sighed, climbing off her bike to run a gloved hand over the tins. 'Do you have any idea what I'd have given for this in the last three years?'

'That makes me sadder than anything else you've told me about being homeless.'

'I didn't think you got sad?'

'It's a rather annoying habit I've been developing. I'm really not happy about it.'

Krystal laughed, crossed the aisle, and opened another pallet. This one contained cardboard boxes filled with gravy thickener. Her sword sliced straight through some of the boxes as she cut the wrap and yellow powder streamed out onto the floor. She giggled and took another swipe, sending powder flying into the air.

Luke turned away. She should be allowed a bit of fun. He wandered around the side of the aisle and stopped dead. What was that? He waited, ears pinned back, and it came again.

'Shush, be quiet a minute.'

Krystal stopped, heeding the tone of his voice. They stood, her with her sword half-raised until the sound came again. It sounded like laughter, only clogged and thick. There were demons who laughed like that. They didn't really know why they were doing it, but they'd learnt it from the people they tortured in Hell and discovered very quickly it was a distinctly unpleasant sound.

He paced silently, raising his sword. His ankle ached from his desperate running to catch Krystal in St Paul's but it stayed solid. Krystal followed, even quieter than he was. Another trait picked up on the streets, perhaps.

He tracked the sound to a door in one side of the warehouse so they sneaked across and peered in through the frosted, fire-reinforced windows. Three zombies sat in a circle on the floor around a low table. In the centre of the table was a packet of white powder with a hole dug in the top. Every now and then, one of the zombies would head butt the bag and stuff their nose or tongue in, emerging with white powder caked across their face.

'That's drugs.' Krystal muttered.

Luke looked at her, eyebrow raised, and she nodded. 'That's coke, or speed maybe. They're doing bloody drugs.'

She covered her mouth and he realised she was laughing. He looked back into the room and had to admit it looked funny. They were taking turns to burst out laughing in that thick, mucus-laden way after they hit the bag.

'Should be easy to kill then. Ready?'

She nodded, sniggered, and raised her sword. He pulled the door slowly open and the smell hit him. He staggered away, clamping his hand over his mouth and nose. Krystal retched, leant over, and spat bile to the floor. It was zombie smell amplified by four days of being shut in a small room. It was worse than that though, something else mingling with the putrescent flesh.

He took a breath and moved back to the open door. That was when he saw the pile. Other zombies had been stacked up in the back corner of the room. He could make out head wounds, where something hard had been used to smash in their skulls. An arm trailed from the pile, gnaw marks clear on the skin, but still ripe with flesh.

They had killed the other zombies and stashed them here. Why? He shook his head and took a step into the room, readying his sword. The zombie facing towards them spotted him and hissed. The others stopped their strange barking and turned, growling. This needed to be fast. He took a step forwards and the zombies reacted.

His eyes widened, but not as quickly as they attacked. The nearest came off its seat and covered the gap between them before he even began to react. It slammed into him and knocked him off his feet. He landed on his elbows, biting his lip as he slammed into the floor, and blood flooded his mouth.

The zombie thrashed and writhed atop him, hands grabbing and tearing at him. Its teeth smashed together inches from his face and sweat broke out on his scalp. He tried to think logically, to approach it sensibly, but its breath crept up his nose and he freaked out, slamming his knees into it and wriggling around. The zombie clung on as he panted and it was all he could do to keep it from eating his face. Again and again it slammed its mouth closed inches from his face, spraying him with filthy saliva.

He was going to die. The thought hadn't ever occurred to him before, not once in thousands of years of life. He was going to die.

The zombie opened its mouth wide and bore down.

Jackson

Jackson sneaked into reception, taking note of the four bodies on the floor. Someone had been busy. Maybe Alex had finally grown some balls. He grinned. If he had, taking the device had been just the right thing to do. He dumped it in the drawer and headed back to the doors.

The zombies had formed their perimeter line outside. He'd need to be beyond that to make this worthwhile. He climbed back in the van and revved the engine. Stupid things didn't even notice until he put his foot down and shot straight for them. Most staggered out the way but he got two and felt their skulls break open against the bumper. Blood flicked up onto the windscreen and he nodded righteously.

He watched in the wing mirrors as the others fell on them and started to feast. He weaved down the street. Why couldn't the damned plague have happened on a Sunday? The city would have been clear of cars, instead of lousy with them. Had Luke even thought about how they were gonna get a bus through all this? Probably not. Bloody amateur.

He kept moving, searching for a quieter part of town. He finally found a closed alleyway and reversed in. There was just room for him to slide out the front door and down the side of the van to the back. The alley was home to a couple of bins and not a lot else. He opened the back of the van and took a step back as the stench escaped

The zombie growled at him, tugging against the restraints. He was glad they were padded. He'd thought it was over the top when he put them in, but the Chinese hadn't liked getting kids with bruises and shit on their arms. Now it was only the padding that stopped the zombie tearing its own hands off.

He stepped closer and grinned as it tried to stand and throw itself at him. Its feet kicked futilely against the restraints. This would be fun. He stepped closer and punched it in the gut. It barely reacted, still growling and snapping its teeth. He pulled his knife from his belt and cut it across the arm. Blood ran out, thin and watery, and still the zombie showed no response.

Damn thing was an alien. Nah, aliens feel pain. Why didn't it feel pain? He grabbed the waistband of its trousers and dragged his knife through it, pulling them off. Its dick was a shrivelled, dead thing. Still, worth a try. He didn't want to get too close so he lashed out with the tip of the blade. It ripped open the bell end and blood sprayed out onto the floor. The zombie hesitated and their eyes met.

There was nothing in them, no sign that he'd just chopped the end off its manhood, but its face twisted, like it was trying to frown.

'What's that? Hurt, does it?'

The zombie growled and he thought it shook its head. He slashed again and there wasn't much left as bits of half-rotted flesh hit the van floor. Again with the frown and again with no other response. If it didn't respond when he chopped its dick off, it wasn't going to respond at all. Unless...

He punched it in the face and, as its head snapped back, he hacked through its throat. Blood geysered and he leapt away, only just avoiding the spray. The sound of its growls changed, becoming thinner and pathetic. He grinned and ran his knife down the side of its face.

Now it really panicked, thrashing around inside the restraints and throwing its head from side to side. They knew what killed them. They knew what to be scared of. He lashed out and hacked its ear off. It screamed, a sound like sandpaper on metal, and he beamed, backing away until he sat on the bench opposite.

'So you get it.' He leant closer, speaking loudly and slowly. 'Stop. Struggling. Or. I'll. Put. This. Knife. Through. Your. Eye.'

It stopped moving, its dull eyes fixed on his. There was a brain in there. It had a brain and it knew what he was saying. He nodded. 'If I let you out the restraints, can you sit still?'

No response. He laughed. 'I'm not going to. You're too screwed. No dick and no ear. Waste of time. But maybe I can train others.'

He nodded and smiled wider. His knife went through its eye while it was still staring at him and it went stiff and slumped in the restraints. He wiped the blade on what was left of its trousers, sheathed it and undid the restraints. The zombie went out in the alley along with all the spare bits of flesh he could kick out. He stared at the corpse for a moment, thinking only one thing. Bait.

He jumped down, grabbed the head and body, then dragged it down the side of the van. There were already zombies gathered outside the alleyway. Dumb fuckers couldn't even get through the gap. He tossed the body out and it landed in a heap with a wet thud. The zombies fell on it and he watched and waited.

One near him looked in good shape, or as near to good shape as zombies got. He lunged, grabbed it around the arms, and dragged it straight back into the gap. Getting it down the side of the van that way was a struggle, and he had to bash it in the face a few times before it settled, but he soon had it around the back of the alley.

He hauled it up and had its hands in restraints before it went really crazy. Catching the legs took a while but he soon had it strapped up. He repeated the punishment to its head until it settled and then he sat back.

'This is simple. I can kill you now. I want to kill you. You're an aberration, a curse upon God's Earth. He wants me to kill you and I do his work. But I think you can be used and God trusts me to make my own judgments. So. I'm going to take the restraints off and you're going to sit still, or I'm going to cut your face off and drag your brains out. Understand?'

Nothing. He took a deep breath and undid one hand and then the other. The creature sat and stared at him and Jackson smiled through gritted teeth. It would work. He could train it. It would go out and kill its mates and he could sit back as they tore one another apart.

This was why God had chosen him. It was like Hen or Li had said. He was thinking big, thinking beyond the immediate future. It was what people did, when they had a world view. He nodded. He had a world view and God knew it.

He undid first one foot and then the other and they sat facing one another, man and zombie. This was the beginning of something, so much larger than—

The zombie lurched at him, teeth bared, and his hand moved before he thought about it. The knife went in its eye and the blood and liquid was warm on his hand. He snarled, opened the back door, and tossed the corpse onto the floor, spitting on it for good measure. He flicked the blood off his hand and onto the body. Damn bastard sneaky thing.

It was smart, smart enough to trick him. But not smart enough to be scared for its own life. It was, he knew, a bad combination. With another growl he leapt out and slammed the back door. He wouldn't give up, not yet. There was potential here.

He turned on the engine and stared at the zombie trying to climb the front of his van. He didn't want to go back to the hospital. Luke and Krystal wouldn't be back till late and when they did they'd still chat and talk and waste time. No one wanted to make decisions.

He'd avoided thinking about the demon all week but he couldn't avoid it any longer. They'd made a deal, of sorts. He was keeping the hostages alive, just like he'd promised, even if he hadn't kept them in St Paul's.

So they were in the hospital, surrounded by devices, and now Luke was going to take them out to the country. God wanted to keep them safe, and Luke was helping with that. But God wanted him, Jackson, to begin the re-population and that wasn't happening. Maybe he should speak to Az about it. Maybe he could recharge the devices at the same time.

He put it in first and put his foot down, smiling at the crunch from beneath his wheels. Stupid bastards.

The reception area was still quiet when he sneaked in. They probably didn't even know he'd left. He headed up the stairs and was about to enter the private room when loud voices drew him to the main room. He poked his head in and found maybe thirty of the ladies in a gaggle, all speaking at once.

They were fine to look at but he'd be so happy if they all shut up. One pulled herself free of the press and approached him. He hadn't bothered learning names, but she was particularly fine, hips swaying back and forth. He should have learnt hers.

'Hi, Jackson, my name's Harriet.' She stuck her hand out and he wrapped it up in his.

'Hi, Harriet. What can I do for you?' She wanted him. Her eyes were telling him quite clearly what he could do for her.

'We're leaving.'

His hand fell away and his mouth opened. For the first time in his life, he didn't have anything to say.

'Can you tell the others please?' She sounded like she was in a church meeting, discussing next week's bake sale. 'We, as a group, feel unable to remain here while Lucifer is part of this. So we are returning to the cathedral where we feel we have a better chance of accomplishing something worthwhile in the new world.'

She turned and stomped away. He watched her arse and found his thoughts turning all sorts of ways. Then what she'd just said sunk in. She was right. Why was he still here? Why was he following Luke? He was a free man but he'd let himself be suckered by the smooth tongue of the great deceiver. God must be furious with him.

He ground his teeth together and approached the group. They quietened, recognising him as the leader already. 'I can't tell the others, I'm coming with you. You're right, how could I be so blind?'

Harriet stepped closer. 'You're coming with us?'

'I am. Unless...' He worked hard to keep the smile from his face. 'You're right about Luke. But the men in St Paul's aren't any better. Trust me, I know. How about we take a couple of the devices and head out on our own?'

Harriet raised a perfect eyebrow and his eyes strayed from her face to her tits where they pushed against her t-shirt. He held his breath.

'We will discuss it. I don't like the thought of returning either so perhaps a new way might be best.'

She turned, dismissing him with a wave of her hand, and he watched her go again. He could watch her go all day. He needed to get ready and collect some devices. He would head down the tunnel, recharge, and speak to Az, then head out somewhere new. Just him and thirty of the hottest women he'd ever met.

He pushed the door open and froze. Bayleigh and Alex stood in the corridor, chatting in hushed voices. He needed to get out of here without them seeing him. Then Alex looked up and raised a hand.

'Hey, Jackson, where've you been? The device is missing from reception. Can we talk to you for a minute?'

Bayleigh

Jackson strolled towards them. He looked casual enough, but his eyes remained fixed on the floor. She was always inclined to believe the best of people, but she struggled with Jackson. She struggled to believe anything good about him at all. The way he looked up, like a kid waiting for his parents to spank him, made it even harder.

How he could look like a little kid when he stood head and shoulders above her she didn't know. But he was up to something. Fortunately, perhaps, Alex spoke first.

'The device has gone from reception and we think the soldiers took it.'

'That's weird. I just checked and it was there.'

'Just? When's just?'

'Like, five minutes ago.'

Bayleigh almost set off down the corridor to check herself. 'You're sure it was there?'

'It was there, alright? I'm not blind.'

Bayleigh held her hands up. 'Hey, easy, it's fine.' What the hell was happening? 'Could Harriet have put it back?'

Alex shrugged. 'Maybe. What was the point of it all though?'

'To get you killed?'

Alex turned pale and put his hand on the wall. 'I don't think so. We're been getting on pretty good. I mean...' He trailed off, blushing, and she did a u-turn in her mind. He was supposed to be the good one, but with one look he'd become just another guy. Nothing unexpected really, but it still hurt. She went to ask about the device again but found different words coming out of her mouth. 'Is she really all that?'

'Uh, well, I mean—'

'She's all that. Trust me, she's fine.' Jackson nodded and smiled as he spoke. Bayleigh could imagine the crude gestures he'd be making with his hands if he thought he'd get away with it. Alex's blush deepened and spread to his forehead. It was half cute and half really annoying.

'Fine, whatever. She wasn't trying to get you killed. So what was the point in stealing it then putting it back?'

'I don't know. I don't think it was her. I know you don't like her, but she wouldn't do that.' Alex sounded like he was pleading. Bayleigh sighed. 'God help me. Being pretty doesn't make you a nice person.'

'Hey, I'm not saying she's a shining example. I'm just saying, I don't think it's in her nature to do something that could get someone else killed.'

Bayleigh harrumphed, but he was quite possibly right. She didn't know Harriet except as an annoyingly pretty woman with an unhealthy interest in God, but she hadn't displayed signs of wanting to kill any of them.

'You're sure it's back in the drawer?'

Jackson curled his upper lip and snarled at her.

'Fine, fine, okay. How about the other four, when did we last check them?' Shrugs all round. 'Right, we check them and meet straight back here. Watch for any zombies that might have come in.'

'There were four dead downstairs, who was that?' Jackson asked. Like it mattered.

Alex raised a hand. 'I did one and Dave did the other three.'

'Dave bagged three zombies? Not bad at all. And you got one. About time.' Jackson patted Alex on the arm and strolled away, smiling broadly. Bayleigh leant close to Alex.

'You know how you feel about him? That's how I feel about Harriet.'

She stalked away before he could reply. Stupid bloody woman with her perfect skin and boobs and every other bloody thing. It didn't matter how pretty she was, she was perfectly capable of being a psycho.

Bayleigh's device was where it should be and still warm. She wandered back to the private room, head spinning as she tried to sort through everything Harriet had said.

Could she really have that much of an issue with someone who'd saved her life? Apparently she could. That alone was worthy of the loathing and annoyance Bayleigh felt towards her. It was selfish and arrogant and those things didn't sit well at all.

She reached the private room first and crept past to the door of the main room. Ten of the ladies were in there, reading magazines or chatting quietly. Sophie sat in the far corner with her feet up on the chair and her knees pressed into her chest. She held her phone at arms length beside her feet.

'Hey, how you doing?' Bayleigh said as she reached her.

'Oh, hi Bayleigh—'

'Call me Bay, if you want.'

'Oh, sure, thanks.'

'Do you know what's going on?'

'Going on?'

'With Harriet and her...' Her what? Gang? Cronies? 'Her group.'

'Oh.' She looked back at her phone and Bayleigh knelt beside her. 'Sophie, I'm worried. If you know what's going on, please tell me.'

Sophie looked at her, big brown eyes that looked ridiculously young pleading with her not to ask.

'Come on. This matters.'

'I think they might have said something about leaving? But I don't know where to or how or anything. I didn't hear that.'

Was she really older than Krystal? Bayleigh sighed and stood. 'Thanks, really.'

She walked away before she could snap at Sophie. It wasn't her fault. It was bloody Harriet's. She'd stirred it all up and now she had some power. Bayleigh knew girls like that. There'd been a few in school and she'd been thrilled the day she left and got away from them. Then she became the boss and forgotten all about them. Yet here she was again.

She left the room, checking faces on the way. She recognised most, all lovely people. But then, all one hundred were lovely people. She was still struggling to find negative things about any of them. Except their perfect skin. That she could bitch about till the cows came home. Except she had no one to bitch about to. Layla would have understood.

Alex was waiting and shook his head as she approached. 'Both still there, both still working.'

'I don't understand. I don't get it—'

'So what's Jackson up to?'

'You saw it too?'

'How could you miss it? For a guy who used to be a criminal, he's got the worst poker face I've ever seen.'

She chuckled and nodded. 'I don't like it when he's up to something.'

'I'm not sure any one does.'

He stopped talking as Jackson rounded the corner. The big man dug his hand in his pocket and pulled a device from it. 'Here's the plan. I'm gonna take two of these into the cavern and charge them up. Then I'll do the same for the other three.'

He walked right by them and Alex, despite his past experience, grabbed his arm. 'You can't do that.'

Jackson spun and Bayleigh in turn grabbed Alex's arm. 'You can't stop him.' She said.

Alex shook her hand away. 'I can and I will. You can't take the devices, it leaves us unguarded.'

'Not any more, mate, not now you've found your inner hunter. You'll be fine.'

He threw him a bright smile and stomped away down the corridor.

'Jackson, wait up, hold up.'

Jackson kept walking and Alex rushed to catch him. 'Alex, be careful, don't do anything stupid.' She called after him.

He waved a hand and said something she didn't catch. She longed to follow, but she had someone else to talk to. She headed into the bedrooms, small hospital rooms with eight beds crammed into each making a raft of mattresses. In the third was Harriet.

She was cramming underwear into a tiny bag and jumped when Bayleigh said her name.

'Where are you going?'

Harriet didn't answer and Bayleigh was about to scramble onto the beds and grab her when she turned and sat amongst the sheets.

'I'm leaving. Some of my sisters are coming with me.'

'Why?'

'You know why.'

'Harriet, where will you go? You can't go back to the soldiers, please tell me you aren't going back there?'

The girl kept her eyes down cast and Bayleigh hissed. 'They'll rape you. You know that, right? They kidnapped you using drugs and kept you unconscious while they unleashed a plague that killed pretty much everyone on Earth.'

She ran out of breath and realised she was panting. 'Tell me you aren't going back there.'

'Where else is there? You just said it, there's nowhere else that's safe.'

'It's safe here.'

'HE'S THE DEVIL. Don't you see that? He's lying to you, it's what he does. Whatever he's told you, it's a lie—'

'He saved my life. And he saved it before that, too, just in a different way. He's not the devil, he's an angel who got a bad reputation.'

Harriet snorted and Bayleigh only just resisted the urge to slap her. 'He can save as many people as he likes, it doesn't change what he is.'

'I don't... I don't understand you.' Bayleigh replied.

'Well then, it's probably a good thing I'm going because I don't understand you either.'

'Stop saying I. How many of you are going?'

'Why does it matter?'

'Because we need a certain number to repopulate and I don't fancy the chances of you being allowed to live after they're done with you.'

Harriet paled and shook her head, lips pressed together in a line. 'I bet he told you that as well.'

She didn't say anything else. She shuffled forward until her legs hung over the edge of the bed then pushed past her and out of the door. Bayleigh watched her go, grinding her teeth together. This was ridiculous. Luke was going to be so pissed off. She was pissed off. How could they be so blind and ungrateful?

She stepped out into the corridor and Alex came racing up, panting. 'He's gone.'

'Already?'

'I followed him down to the car park. He wouldn't listen, just grabbed the back door device and headed straight down the tunnel.'

Bayleigh was about to speak when Alex glanced over her shoulder and, muttering 'see you', brushed past her. She spun, already knowing what she'd see but still moaning in frustration when she did. Harriet was half-in and half-out a doorway, beckoning to him with a dimply smile that made Bayleigh want to punch her. They spoke for a moment before disappearing into the room together.

Bayleigh squeezed her eyes closed and blinked back the tears. She should feel tired, but she didn't. Her brain hurt but her body was still on that weird high. She could run to the river and back right now and not break a sweat. Luke had warned her it might run out and to be ready for the comedown, but there were no signs of it yet.

Where was Dave? Did it matter? He wasn't good for much either way. She just wanted Luke to come back and take control. She hated thinking that, hated the weakness in her. But she wasn't weak, not really. This was something she'd never imagined before. No one person could handle it, not alone. Why did she feel alone?

She pushed through the door into the private room. Ed stood at the window, head resting on his folded arms. She joined him watching the zombies come and go. That was when she spotted the van.

'Where did the van come from?'

'Dunno. Been there since I came back in here.'

Bayleigh frowned. She watched it for a while before deciding no one was getting out.

'How're you doing?'

'M'okay. Bored. You?'

She sighed. 'Frustrated.'

'Worse things to be.'

She glanced down at the top of his head and smiled. 'That's very true. I could be dead—'

'Or a zombie.'

'Or a zombie. Small mercies, huh?'

He nodded and watched and she watched with him. She registered the door opening and Alex shuffling in. He joined them by the window, hands shoved deep in his pockets. She glanced over at him and he gave her a sheepish smile.

'You going with her, then?'

'Of course not. She's a bit of a bitch, if I'm honest.'

She smiled and went back to staring. When it came, the scream was unbelievably loud and such a shock she only just stopped short from wetting herself. She raced from the room, Alex thudding along behind her. She'd outdistanced him when the scream came again.

The room was right on the edge of the safety field and the door swung open as she pushed it. She got a flash of what lay beyond, of blood on white sheets and someone's face with the eyes gouged out, before the door swung back.

Krystal

It was like watching a movie in fast forward. One moment the zombies were gathered around the coke, the next they were hurtling towards them. The first was on Luke before she had a chance to think. The other two were only marginally slower and she raised her sword enough for one of them to run itself through. She felt the blade burst out its back as it arms closed around her and its mouth lunged for her face.

She snapped her head back and the teeth clashed together just short. Then she bashed her forehead into the creature's nose. It growled and she did it again. Its arms left her shoulders and she butted it for a third time, putting everything she had into it. She bashed its cheekbone as it turned its head and the world spun as she felt it crack.

The creature thrashed around on her sword and she jumped away, yanking it as hard as she could. It came out like a fiver from a rich man's wallet, so she had to take more steps and keep pulling. The zombie fell back and finally it tore free.

The third had been dithering, making strange chucking noises, but it decided now was its time and rushed her. She dashed to one side and it grabbed her sleeve. She hacked its wrist and its hand was left hanging from her jacket. She smacked the hand with the sword hilt, trying to ignore the urge to scream and flap her arms. She broke it off, but by then the creature was back, shoving its bleeding stump in her face.

She opened her mouth to scream, and shut it just as it bashed her in the jaw. She kept her lips pressed together, protection against the blood smeared on her cheeks and chin. The zombie finally got its arm out of the way and dived in, teeth snapping. Her sword was trapped between them, pointing at the ceiling. Just before the thing bit her face off, she thrust straight up. It went in through the soft underside of its mouth and broke out the front of its forehead.

It sounded like someone throwing an apple at the ground really hard. She waited for it to go stiff but it didn't. Her sword was yanked from her hands as it staggered away across the room. The first zombie, bleeding profusely from its broken face and gut wound, came charging back. She was defenceless.

Krystal grabbed its hands and the two of them danced across the room. Somehow she kept her feet and kept the zombie at bay. Then her back hit the wall and it charged, mouth wider than should have been possible. She had a moment before the jaws closed around her neck, and in that moment she saw the pile of dead.

She twisted, escaping the jaws, and the weight of her attacker pushed her down the wall until her foot caught the first corpse. It was now or never. She let go of its hands and dropped into a crouch. The zombie came crashing onto her but in the split second she had, she grabbed an arm and hauled it from the pile.

It came free and she shook with relief. Then the full weight of the zombie landed on her and she tumbled over. She lay among the bodies, smothered in the stench of rotting flesh, feeling them shift and give way beneath her. She wanted more than anything to scream and wail, but she could feel the blood dried around her mouth. She didn't dare open it.

She wriggled and writhed and got free from beneath the zombie. For a brief moment they lay side by side, ready to make out. Then she heaved herself up until she knelt above it. It reached for her, mouth opening again.

With all the strength she possessed she raised her stolen arm and drove it straight down into the creature's mouth. The rough bone thrusting out the end went straight through the back of its mouth, tearing out its throat and severing its tongue.

It thrashed. One hand smacked her in the side of the face and sent her flying. She landed on the ground beside the pile of dead and glanced about her.

The zombie she'd stabbed was still in the corner of the room, helplessly fumbling with the sword stuck through its face. Luke was on his back, his attacker clawing and grabbing at his face as its teeth drew nearer and nearer. She looked again at the pile of dead and spotted a tool belt on one dressed. Most of it was buried, but she grabbed the belt and heaved. The body came out far enough for her to explore the pouches strapped to it.

A long screwdriver hung down and she grabbed it with a silent 'yes!' She took three steps to where Luke was defending himself and rammed the screwdriver straight into the back of the zombie's skull. It twitched and went still. Luke heaved it off with a roar and lay on his back, staring up at her. She gave him a nod.

She'd saved him. She'd just saved an angel. She grinned and went flying as the zombie, still gagging on the arm bone protruding from its mouth, barrelled into her. She hit the floor and kept rolling, praying it kept her out of the creature's reach. It wasn't coming for her, though. Luke was back in the same position, the zombie astride him clawing and snapping.

It was the best thing that could have happened. The screw driver went in nice and easy and it joined its friend on the floor. This time Luke jumped to his feet and they faced the remaining zombie together.

It was almost comical, the way its hands flapped at the sword handle. The one time she saw it get hold, it pushed the wrong way and the sword went deeper through its face. Luke picked his sword off the floor and stepped closer. The zombie clearly wasn't paying any attention and paid even less when he chopped the back third of its head off.

The skull cracked and came off in bits, and the brain poured out like thick rice pudding. It was the last straw. She could handle rolling in dead zombies, but the brains were just too much. Krystal stumbled to the corpse corner and vomited. Her sick rained down onto the corpses and the smell got even worse. She couldn't stop, sweaty hands clutching her jeans as she bent double.

Luke took her shoulders and led her out of the room. The air felt like coming home, like cold water on a hot day, and she collapsed against the wall, sliding down to sit. Luke sat beside her and she was gratified to see his own face covered in sweat.

'You saved my life.' He sounded surprised.

'Uh, yeah, whatever.'

'Thank you. It's the first time.'

Krystal laughed. 'Hopefully the last. Doesn't happen all that often, you know.'

He shrugged. 'Maybe more so now. Thanks.'

'It's fine. Least I could do. You wanna explain what happened in there?'

'Drugs. Whatever it was on the table set them off.'

'It's scary. I mean, they can change that much.'

Luke rose to his feet. 'It is. I'd assumed they move the way they do because their bodies were no longer strong enough to do anything else but that isn't true. If something gets hold of them like that stuff did, they can move... well, you saw them.'

'Oh yeah I did. That's some scary shit.'

He offered her a hand and pulled her up. Leaving her brushing herself down and spitting to clear her mouth of vomit, he went back into the room. She would be happy to never go in there again but the thought of her sword had her stepping reluctantly closer. Luke emerged bearing the bag of white powder in one hand and her sword in the other and she breathed a long sigh of gratitude.

He pulled the door closed behind him. 'I'm never going in there again.'

She chuckled and cleaned then sheathed her sword. In the meantime, Luke was staring at the drugs.

'What?' She asked.

'I'm wondering if we can put this to use.'

'Normally you just put it up your nose. I'm not sure that's a good idea, though. I mean, it's tempting, but I don't think we'd be very safe.'

'No, no, not us. I mean with the zombies. Would turning them into that,' he waved a hand at the room, 'help us somehow?'

'Hmm, let me think. Shall we make the zombies more dangerous?' She gave him a look she hoped expressed her disgust for the notion and he nodded sadly.

'I think you're right. Down the toilet, then.'

She stared at the bag as he walked away. What was the street value of that stuff? A month ago she'd have killed for a bag of coke that big. Not to take but to sell. She could have stayed in a hotel for a couple of weeks, bought some new clothes. Now they were flushing it down the toilet.

Luke returned a couple of minutes later without the bag and gestured around the warehouse. 'We're happy it's got what we want?'

'Yeah, think so. Enough to survive on.'

'Great. Shall we grab something to eat before we head back?'

She nodded and they ambled around the warehouse until they found stuff they didn't need to heat up. They sat in the centre of the enormous space eating from tins and jumping at every creak and rattle that reached them. They finished fast and, with a lump in her gut from cold sausage and beans, Krystal strolled back towards the front door.

The quiet was blissful. She could stay in here all day, drinking it up, if it wasn't for the feeling that at any moment some coked-up zombie was going to emerge from hiding and bite her face off.

They wheeled the bikes back out and wound through the housing estate, dodging zombies as they went. It reminded her of where she and Ed had spent the night. It was far creepier than the city. There were two elderly zombies in macs and walkers creeping side by side down the street. They probably thought they were heading for church. They certainly showed no signs of knowing they were zombies. Until the rumble of bikes made one turn, fix its dark eyes on her, and bare its teeth.

She gunned the bike and rode on. They passed a green space with swings where kids were still playing. One lay beneath the swings, legs twisted where it must have come off and broken them. Another of the children looked up from where it chewed its playmate's arm, blood running down its jaws. Its eyes fixed on her as well. They were eyes that should have been too big for its face, the eyes of a child, but they were sunken just like the old lady's.

She turned away and fixed her gaze on the back of Luke's bike, determined to keep it there until they reached the main road.

She let out a sigh of relief when they did and rolled up next to him as he paused at the top of the slip road. He lifted his visor. 'Are you alright?' He asked.

'Yeah, think so. That was pretty horrible.'

'It's almost as though the plague never came to them.'

'Except for the children eating children bit.'

'Oh no, I've seen that before.'

She shuddered and nodded north down the road. Luke lowered his visor, gunned his bike, and was replaced by a piece of flying metal. She thought for a moment he'd been cut in half. Then she thought nothing as a wave of heat and sound washed over her and threw her into darkness.

Alex

He wasn't far behind Bayleigh when they reached the door, but he missed whatever it was that made her back away, hands raised in defence. He slipped by and pushed through the door. A pair of sightless eyes stared at him from the bed. Only they didn't stare because there were no eyeballs, only empty red sockets.

His gorge rose and he pressed his lips together, swallowing as saliva flooded his mouth. He made himself step into the room, which was when he noticed her. Another of the ladies was behind the door, shaking hands pressed against her cheeks. Alex knelt in front of her, blocking the view on the bed, and put his arms around her. She pressed her face into his chest and shuddered until something snapped and she burst into tears.

He stayed there until his knees burned with the effort, then lifted her to her feet and guided her to the door. She went willingly enough, running from the room with a choked sob. She was replaced by Bayleigh, who was accompanied by an out-of-breath-

Harriet. The three of them stood around the bed, none of them speaking. He didn't know what to say.

He tried to approach it from a scientific point of view. Objectively, one of the ladies was dead. Her blouse was open and there were red marks on her breasts. Her eyes were... as he came around the side of the bed he saw her eyes, or what was left of them, smeared on the sheets beside her. He swallowed again.

Her eyes had been gouged out. He couldn't yet see why she was dead, unless it was the shock alone, which was by no means unlikely.

'What happened?' Harriet's voice carried none of her usual assuredness. It shook as much as she did and he went back around the bed to put his arm around her shoulders. She snuggled into him and shook harder.

'I don't know.' He looked over her head at Bayleigh, eyebrows raised, and she shrugged in return. She lifted the lady's hand and checked her pulse. She only held it a moment before she rested it back on the sheet. She leant over the bed, then stiffened and backed away.

He extricated himself from Harriet and joined Bayleigh. As he leant over, she pointed into the eye socket. What he'd thought were just sockets were, in fact, deep pits. Whoever had gouged her eyes out had driven the weapon deep into her brain. He held his breath and leant closer, looking for signs of what the weapon might have been.

He wasn't surprised when he found tearing in the skin around the eyes, as though the murderer had been using something small and sharp. Or their nails. He glanced at Bayleigh. She was white as a sheet and chewing on her own nails.

'Any ideas?' He asked.

She shook her head, gaze fixed on the woman's face. Alex led Harriet out the room, still swallowing saliva. He had a very good idea who did it, but for some reason he didn't want to say. There was loyalty among the seven of them, despite Jackson being a... actually, there was no loyalty for Jackson, but Alex felt something for Dave.

Mostly, it was sympathy. The guy had been screwed over by whatever Luke did to him, but he was trying. The new emotionless Dave was creepy, but he wasn't a murderer. Except Alex couldn't get the image from his mind of Dave slamming the zombie's face into the floor until it broke. He needed to find him.

He led Harriet to where some of the other ladies were huddled together. He wanted to say something, to clear the air after their conversation of earlier. Harriet had dragged him into one of the rooms and told him in a breathy voice she wanted to make love to him. It should have been a wonderful moment, except the next line out of her mouth was that he had to leave with them when they went.

He'd tried to talk her around to not going, at which point she'd called him a using bastard, which was rich coming from her. He bit his tongue, though, and tried to make it better, but she'd snapped that if he cared about her, he'd stay with her to make sure she was okay. He'd said he wanted to stay and look after everyone else as well and she'd sneered. He'd left then. He and Lisa had argued from time to time, but he'd always been good at shutting up when the right moment came.

Now as he removed his arm from her shoulder and she gave him a grateful look, he knew this was the right moment for something. Except he didn't know what the something was, so he just smiled and headed back to the room. He met Bayleigh as she came out.

'He stuck his fingers through her eyes.' She blurted at him.

'He?'

'Any women here strong enough to do that?'

'I don't think you have to be all that strong. And there are a lot more women here than men.'

Bayleigh sniffed and wrinkled up her nose. 'Either way, it's a sick, twisted thing to do.'

'Yeah. Do you think the attacker opened her blouse or was it already open?'

'Does it matter?'

'Well it's just whether they were doing something together and then it changed or—'

'So what, they were going to have sex so it's her fault he killed her?'

'God, no, what are you talking about? I just meant, if they were in there and doing something already, it would take much less effort to have done it.' He shuddered and swallowed.

'Was she gay?' Bayleigh said.

'We can ask.'

'Right, because all those lovely Christian girls are going to know or even admit to one of them being gay.'

He leant against the door frame and rubbed his eyes. 'This is horrible. The world's full of zombies and we're doing their job for them.'

He could feel Bayleigh's eyes burning in to him and met her gaze as she spoke. 'You think you know who did it, don't you?'

He shrugged and walked past her into the room. She'd pulled the sheet up to cover the corpse and he walked past the bed to the window. 'I don't want to say in case I'm wrong.'

'Or right, right?'

'Yeah.'

'Was it Dave?'

'I... I don't know. Just, after seeing him fight the zombies in reception... he was feral, completely off the rails. He could have done this and not even know he did it.'

'But why?'

'Dunno. That's why I'm not saying anything, because what's his motive?'

'We should find him.'

There was no avoiding it so he brushed past her and out the door. An inspection of the rooms within the field turned up nothing so they split up and began to explore the hospital. Even knowing it as well as they did, it was going to take hours. If he had a mobile they could at least have phoned him, but he'd never got another after throwing his off the miniature St Paul's.

Alex started in the children's ward, shivering as he walked through the now-empty rooms. Jackson and Luke had cleared this one and he'd been pathetically grateful he hadn't needed to go with them. Now the silence was almost as bad.

Room by room he trawled the hospital, not finding Dave and not really expecting to. So where the hell had he gone? Had he realised what he'd done and run away? Maybe he'd gone outside to die. Maybe he'd gone the same way as Jackson and headed back to the soldiers. He could be looking to them to take him in, which would be bad news. He knew what the group were doing and planning.

Alex snarled and headed back to the ward. The sound of the ladies reached him long before he stepped off the stairs and he slowed, trying to gauge the mood. There was anger and tears, predictable considering the circumstances. Harriet's voice carried loud over everyone else.

'This is the reason you asked me to give you. You needed a reason to leave and here it is. These people are murderers. Luke claims he went to find food, but what's to say he's not right here, waiting for his next victim? We all know the girl is on his side.'

Alex stalked down the corridor and shoved through the women, ignoring their cries of protest until he came face to face with Harriet. She started to smile at him until he opened his mouth.

'You don't like Luke, and that's fine. But don't use the death of anyone to make your political point. Ever. That's a crappy thing to do and you know it. This wasn't Luke. What we need to do is work out who it was and how to keep everyone safe. So why not put your brain to use doing that instead of causing hysteria in a place that's already far too close to it.'

He left a silence in his wake as he stormed off. His hands were shaking. He'd spent the last four years of his life buried in the lab and the thought of speaking like that to anyone was ridiculous. He found himself smiling as he reached the private room. He shoved the door open and froze.

Ed and Dave were sat on the two beds, chatting to one another. They both raised a hand in greeting then went right on talking. He stood and stared for a minute, blinking. They were talking about computer games, Call of Duty from the sounds of it. He'd never been a role-player, he enjoyed Mortal Kombat far too much.

He strolled over, trying to calm the churning in his gut, and sat in one of the chairs. He tried to get in a position where he could get Ed out quick if he needed to. His machinations made them break off the conversation and look at him.

'Hi, Alex, are you alright?' Ed asked.

'Yeah, well, you know, apart from the obvious.'

'Well yeah, zombies and all that.'

Alex blinked and felt sweat pop out on his forehead. They hadn't told Ed. He'd been in here the entire time. 'God, Ed, you don't know. One of the ladies was murdered.'

He thought to keep his eyes on Dave's face and was rewarded by a look of complete stunned surprise. There was no chance it was acting. The guy didn't even express his own feelings anymore, let along fake ones. He really didn't know.

Ed was pale and shaking his head. 'What happened?'

Alex spared as many of the details as he could and kept it short. When he'd finished, Ed's first question was whether it could have been a zombie. Dave's were whether it could have been Jackson. Alex hadn't gone there, maybe because he was so convinced it was Dave, but now he had no choice.

'Yeah. I don't think it was a zombie, there was nothing eaten. But Jackson? Yes, I suppose so.'

The three of them exchanged looks. When the door slammed open they all jumped. Bayleigh stared at Dave, then at Alex, who shrugged. 'I don't think so. He didn't know.'

She stalked across the room and grabbed Dave's hand. He watched her, frowning in confusion as she inspected his nails. Alex got a look and saw the lack of damage and blood beneath them. He didn't do it, which meant it had to be Jackson. It had to be.

'We wait.' Alex said. 'He comes back with the devices and we take him.'

Ed snorted. 'You take him how? He's bigger that all of us put together.'

'Dave could handle him.'

Dave had remained silent until now, but he looked at him with those weird flat eyes and shook his head. 'I know what you said about the zombies, but I can't just switch it on. I don't even know what it is. I don't know what it feels like.'

'How can you not know?'

When Dave spoke again, there was something odd about his voice. It was almost as though he was trying to sound like someone who was sad might sound. But he was trying instead of just being. There was no real emotion there, but his voice cracked in all the right places, and Alex found himself rethinking things again.

'I don't know what anything feels like. It's all gone.'

Alex and Bayleigh shared a look and Alex nodded to the door. They excused themselves and headed out. When they reached the door, Bayleigh hesitated. 'Um, Ed, I think one of the ladies wants to speak to you.'

It was as poor an attempt as Alex had ever heard, but if Dave realised, he didn't show it. He raised a hand in farewell to Ed and leant back in his chair. Alex pulled the door closed and dragged the others down the corridor. 'It could still be him. I know he seems innocent, but I think he's acting.'

'I don't know what he's doing. I don't have a clue anymore. I was so sure it was him, but now...'

'Ed, how long have you guys been talking?'

'Dunno, half hour maybe.'

'He didn't get very long to clean himself up if he did do it.' Alex said.

Bayleigh shook her head. 'It depends how long the body was there.'

'Not long. She was still warm.'

Bayleigh looked at the floor, blinking furiously. Alex patted her shoulder, aware of how shallow a gesture it was but not having anything better.

She rubbed her eyes. 'So he got cleaned up in record time and can add being an amazing actor to his freaky new persona?'

'It's that or Jackson came back out the tunnel after I left, made it up to the ward with no one noticing, killed the woman and got back downstairs, covered in blood, again with no one noticing.'

Ed raised a hand. 'Unless...' They waited for him to speak. 'Unless one of the other ladies did it.'

'Why do you think that?'

Alex nodded. Bayleigh was good with him, always giving him her attention and not ignoring what he said. And in this instance, Alex thought he might have a point.

'I heard two of them talking.'

Alex and Bayleigh leant closer at the same time and Ed gave them an uneasy look. 'It wasn't much, I just heard one saying they needed to take someone out of action while they got out. But I don't know who they were taking out of action or anything really.'

Alex put his hand to his brow and massaged it. His head hurt. 'Let me just check. The words they used were 'take someone out of action.'

'Well not exactly. They said something like 'she's gonna do it because she likes sex.' His cheeks went red and he looked at the floor. 'Didn't want to mention it because of, you know...'

Alex patted him on the shoulder, a gesture for all occasions it appeared, and made eye contact with Bayleigh. Ed hadn't known about the open blouse. So now there were three suspects, and he hadn't the first idea what to do with any of them.

Jackson

He slipped through the darkness, God's messenger following his calling. That he was on his way to speak to a demon was making him less comfortable than he would have liked. But he couldn't deny they both had the same goal in mind. Saving the ladies and bringing life back to God's Earth. That was the only thing worth focusing on and he hadn't seen much of it from Luke.

Luke was all about getting safe. Getting himself safe and anyone who wanted to come along. It was like rescuing the hostages had fulfilled his duty and now he just wanted the quiet life. But what was he going to do, impregnate every one of them? They needed variety. He wasn't a scientist like Alex, but even he knew if all the kids came from the same father, the next generation would be screwed up.

So what was Luke going to do? Take them out to the country and keep them there until they were old and dried up? Jackson sneered in the darkness. The conflict within was lessening with every step he took. They needed to repopulate and there was no other way to do it than use every man here and every woman. If Luke had his way, Earth was doomed.

He wasn't working with the demon. He was just keeping up to date, keeping their footsteps aligned so they reached the same destination. He sneered again, this time at his own words, words that sounded fancy but meant nothing. He'd never used those kind of words before. It was probably his bible reading. He'd finished it this morning and felt considerably wiser than he had. There were passages he recognised, things Mam had read to him, but there was plenty he didn't.

The old testament was brutal. It made him realise his methods were justified. What he was doing was way nicer than half the stuff the people who came before did. He was a saint compared to some of that stuff.

He emerged into the cavern and paused. The lights were dim, only a couple of torches still alight, which suited him just fine. He crept around the wall until the shadows joined it to the cathedral then sneaked around it until he reached the entrance.

Jackson peered in. The church was silent and empty, the only light cast by the torches that sent flickers through the stained glass. He slipped through the door and down one side of the pews, staying deep in the shadows. He drew level with the machine and paused. A huge cross hung above the altar and, though he knew he wouldn't answer, he sat at the end of the pew and prayed.

He prayed and prayed and waited and prayed a bit more. He heard nothing, but God trusted him. He knew that. He shifted and stood, knees cracking.

'No one answering?'

He jumped and looked sideways at Az. How had the hell did he do that? 'Didn't see you there.'

'People often say that. Normally it's just after they've murdered someone. Murdered anyone recently, Jackson?'

He shook his head. He shouldn't be here. He shouldn't be talking to Az. He was a demon, the incarnation of evil on Earth. But he didn't know how to do God's work without help, and God wasn't speaking to him.

'Yeah, he must be busy.' Jackson said.

'Hmm?'

'God. He must be busy.'

'He's always busy, but if you listen hard, you can still hear him. His answers are in the world around you. You can hear him speak in the trees and in the wind, in the roar of the sea and the silence of the mountains.'

'Really?'

'Nah, I'm just shitting you. He's a lazy bastard and no mistake.'

Jackson's hands tightened into fists and his lip curled. He shouldn't be here. He shouldn't be listening to this *thing* talk about God like that. 'Respect your betters.'

Az chuckled a deep rumble that came from his gut. 'If I have any betters, I've yet to meet them. Don't get me wrong, he's got plenty more power than me and a touch more experience, too, but I'm down here having a ball, and he's trying to manage a realm in revolt.'

'What?'

'Oh nothing, don't let it worry you. He's busy, let's leave it at that. Now, what can I do for you?'

'How do you know I came here for you?'

'Why else would you come?'

Jackson felt the devices crammed in his pocket and kept his mouth closed. The demon leant closer and Jackson shifted on the pew, but glared back at him. He'd never met anyone he had to look up to, but Az towered above him even when they were sitting. Jackson stood and leant against the stone pillar that met the end of the pews.

'I don't know what to do. The ladies, some of the ladies, want to leave Luke.'

Az clapped his hands together, fierce smile spreading across his savage face. He waved for Jackson to continue. 'They wanted to come back here, but I'm not delivering them into the hands of anyone, not you or the soldiers. But then...'

His fists were clenched so tight his wrists ached. 'But then, without the soldiers, who's going to fuck them? I can't do it all by myself, the next genera-tion'll be mutants.'

Az nodded, deep lines forming on his forehead over a mouth pursed in thought. 'I'm glad you've thought about this. What have you suggested to them?'

'I've said I'll take them somewhere else. We'll find somewhere safe and away from everyone.'

'And then you'll have your fun.'

Jackson snarled, cheeks heating up as he shook his head. 'That's what I just said. I can't, not if we're going to repopulate.'

'That does leave you in a quandary, doesn't it.'

Az leant back, steepling his fingers and resting one massive leg on the other as he stared up at the cross. 'This, you know, is the biggest joke of all.' He nodded at the cross. 'This whole son of god thing. You know who the real son of god is?'

Jackson growled. Az went on as though he hadn't. 'Lucifer. He's the real son, but Christians didn't like the idea of a wayward son, so they in-vented some other rubbish to make them feel bet-ter. Same with lots of the others too. People stealing other people's heads and such. All a crock.'

Jackson stalked away across the cathedral, not car-ing whether Az was watching. He knelt beside the machine, found the hanging plugs and plugged in his devices. Moments later they buzzed and he pulled them out and shoved them in his pocket.

Az still stared up at the cross, eyebrows together as he frowned. Jackson was halfway up the aisle when Az spoke. 'I'll bring them to you.'

Jackson paused, one foot half raised. He set it down and stared up at the dome. It was beautiful, even in miniature. Nothing close to the majesty of God, but still. He'd never thought about beautiful before. Beautiful was a fine pair of tits on the woman kneeling in front of you. Beautiful was cash in large amounts. God was teaching him all the time. Just because he didn't speak to him out loud didn't mean he wasn't learning.

Jackson turned back to the demon. He acted all tough but there was truth, hidden in his words and behind his sneer. He stomped back to the front pew and lowered himself onto it.

'Who will you bring?'

'I'll bring soldiers. Not all of them, just those I can rely on not to blab to Etienne and the others. They can take turns, it won't take long. We can do it in secret.' Az nodded and brought his eyes around to stare at Jackson. 'Can you do that? Can you be secret?'

'I'm here, aren't I?'

'And does anyone know you're here?'

'They think I'm charging the devices.'

'Okay, then.' Az paused, his eyes fixed on Jackson's. 'Tell me, how is Dave doing?'

'Alright. Dunno. He's quiet.'

'But nothing weird happening?'

'Nah.'

'Mmm.'

'How will you know where I've gone?'

'I'll find you, don't worry about that. But Jackson, stay in the city, yeah? Don't go gallivanting around the countryside. I don't like the country.'

Jackson nodded and rose from the pew. There was a burning in his gut and he didn't know whether it was nerves at the reality before him or a loathing for the creature sat on the bench. Was he betraying God? God had created demons, hadn't he? Az was his creature, just the same as the rest. He shook his head and didn't look back until he left the cathedral.

He slipped back into the ward and replaced the devices. It was quieter than when he left. He would get the other devices and get it done, but he wanted to speak with Harriet and check they were still coming with him. He grabbed the other two devices, shoved them in his pocket and went in search of her.

He spotted her figure long before he saw her face and paused for a moment. She'd be his. She had child-bearing hips and tits he couldn't wait to sink his teeth into. It was as though she heard him thinking, because she turned from the two ladies she was chatting with to stare at him. She might have seen him flush as she swayed over, but he didn't care. If it had just been the two of them, he'd have got his dick out there and then and showed her what she was missing.

'Jackson. Where have you been?'

'Charging the devices, getting ready to leave. Are you ready?'

She bit her lip in a way that made him stiffen, and nodded. 'We are. Where are we going?'

'That's what we gonna talk about. We'll stay in London. There's food here and everything else we need. How many of you are there?'

'There are forty two of us who want to go.' She glanced around, eyes narrowed. 'Forty two true believers out of a hundred. I struggle to believe the church allow that many to be so lax in their worship.'

'They don't understand.' He stepped closer to her, feeling her breath on his neck. She didn't step away and he raised enough lip to show her some teeth. 'They aren't true believers, because they don't understand the majesty of God. They don't know he's there, they only think he is. Until they know, they'll never believe.'

She nodded vehemently, hands clasped together. 'I think we've chosen the right person to go into partnership with.'

He let the partnership comment pass. It was fine, if she wanted to think that. She'd soon learn who the boss was. She was a believer but she didn't see her place in the plan. None of them did, because none of them saw the big picture.

'We need a safe house for fifty people, somewhere close enough to the hospital supplies in case we need them. I'm going to charge the other devices. When I get back I want you to be ready and have found a place. Understand?'

Her face creased slightly but smoothed just as quickly. Perhaps she was just beginning to see who was in charge here. She nodded. 'We'll be ready.'

'Good.' For a moment he thought about kissing her, but he wouldn't stop at that. He settled for an arm on her shoulder. She didn't flinch away and he took that as a good sign. He stomped out the room and jogged down to reception. He'd got even fitter in the last week than he'd been before. The constant moving and fighting and running had toned the bits he might not have bothered with, and the last four days of sleep had got him rested.

He plucked the device from the drawer, shoved it in his pocket with the other two, and turned to go. Bayleigh and Alex stepped out from where they'd been hiding and stood in front of the stairs.

'Hi, Jackson. Tell me, exactly, what you've been doing for the last two hours.'

Luke

The piece of metal hit him like a truck. He was utterly unprepared, which was the only thing that saved his life. The human body can withstand a massive impact, so long as it's relaxed enough, and he was as relaxed as he could be, considering the circumstances. He flew like he hadn't in the three weeks since he'd come to Earth, and hit the concrete shoulder first. Something gave way, like his ankle had in the cavern, then he rolled, gravel spitting up against his visor as his helmet bashed against the floor.

He slid the last few feet and shredded the skin off his hands. He lay still as warmth flooded in. He tried to lift his head, but nothing worked. Even his hands, wet with blood, refused to move. He rolled onto his side, getting there through a series of puppy-weak pushes with his good arm. The pain in his shoulder flared like someone had stabbed him and he blacked out.

He came back seconds later, blinking furiously. The warmth still lapped at him and he couldn't breathe. He tried to take his helmet off but his bad shoulder refused to budge, so he flipped the visor up with one hand and sucked in air. Smoke flooded his lungs and he burst out coughing, rolling onto his front. Saliva dripped onto the tarmac as his hacking got worse and worse. Tears streamed down his face.

Forehead pressed into the ground, he pushed himself to his knees. He stared across the tarmac and saw flames and pieces of debris before he scrunched his eyes shut against the smoke. Hands grabbed him and he tried to shake the zombie off. It was going to bite him. He was going to die because of a damned explosion, He couldn't die here, not like this, it—

'Stop it, bloody stop it and get up. Come on.'

Krystal's voice, low and rough and coarse, was like a choir, and he stopped struggling, head still resting on the concrete. But she was still pulling at him. Why was she pulling at him? He needed sleep, not movement.

'Get up get up get up.' She thumped him on the back and he roused himself enough to understand that they needed to move, quickly. She put a hand beneath his right shoulder and he screamed, blushing at the sound.

'Other side, other side.' He didn't sound like himself. He sounded like he'd been smoking forty a day for a few hundred years, but she understood. She grabbed his left arm and shoulder and heaved, and he tried his best to join in. He gained his feet and together they weaved a few steps until the smoke thinned. Her hands went away and he swayed, opening his eyes fully.

They were beside a car and Krystal opened the passenger door. She half turned back when a figure lunged from the car, hands clutching at her. She tripped over herself, into him, and they tumbled to the concrete. The zombie lurched straight past and took a moment to turn and face them.

Krystal awkwardly drew her sword, elbow digging into his stomach, and held it before her. The zombie came at them and she shifted, grinding his ankle into the floor where she sat on it. He suppressed the groan of pain, focusing on the creature.

It fell on them, but Krystal had the sword ready and it entered its mouth. The zombie kept coming and the blade erupted from the back of its head. Blood streamed down the blade and over Krystal's hands as the zombie's head oozed down it and thumped into her lap.

They were still for a second before Krystal shouted and shoved the zombie off, flailing at it until she could stand. Luke watched her, half-amused and half sickened by the dead creature. Krystal got control of herself and grabbed her sword. She put her foot on the zombie's face and yanked the blade free, then wiped it on the creature's clothing.

She tossed the sword in the open car door and returned to him. She hauled him upright and shoved him in the car. She slammed the door, raced around to the other side, and climbed in.

They sat for a moment, side by side, staring at the chaos in front of them. Then in unison they jumped and twisted in their seats to explore the back. There was nothing there and they turned back, letting out long breaths.

He still struggled to breathe and another pain made itself known, like someone was jabbing him in the chest with pins. He felt it gingerly and found a rib that sent sharp shards of pain through his body. He'd broken a rib. Probably. His observations had never gone as far as exploring wounds. He'd never had wounds.

He tried to ignore it, focusing instead on the wreckage before them. They faced the petrol station they had used before they went to the warehouse. Where the station had been was now a raging fire and the vague skeleton of the shop. The street around them was covered in pieces of blackened and twisted metal and in some places, the smoke was still too thick to see through.

The afternoon sunlight was strong and burned through the smoke, casting random, shifting shadows on the floor. He shifted in his seat and almost cried out as his shoulder turned. He slumped back and contented himself with turning his head to look at Krystal.

'It blew up.' It was as inane a comment as he could have made and he blushed. She nodded, eyes wide as she stared into the smoke.

'Yeah. Wow.'

They sat in silence as Luke tried to organise his thoughts. There were things they needed to do. He had to work out how they were getting home, but every time he tried, he took a breath and the pain swamped him. After a few minutes, Krystal turned in her seat to look at him. Her nose was bloody and her face was covered in dust and dirt. He probably looked the same.

'We need to get back to the hospital. Can you ride?'

She sounded so calm and so assured he almost burst into tears. He ground his teeth together. He hadn't cried in thousands of years. Had he ever cried? All it took now was a broken rib and a bit of pride. He sniffed. Thousands of years of punishment and now he had the capacity to feel something other than delight in pain. He wasn't sure how disappointed he was in himself. The Father told him he deserved this and at the time he'd thought it was punishment. Now, though...

He chuckled and shook his head at Krystal's frown of confusion. 'Sorry, there's really nothing funny, just thinking about how nice it is to feel a broken rib.'

She prodded him in the chest and he gasped, eyes watering. 'Yeah, looks nice. Can you ride?'

He groaned and shook his head. 'Not yet. My shoulder's gone.'

'Gone?'

'I don't think it's broken. I don't know really. Maybe give it a day and it'll be fine.'

Krystal nodded, turned to the front, and put her seat belt on. 'You might want yours on, too. Ed was never very keen on my driving.'

Luke managed a smile and did his belt left handed, which was considerably more difficult that he expected. He was still struggling to plug it in when Krystal turned the key. The motor turned over a few times and stopped. She did it again and again and nothing happened.

'Shit, dammit.' She slammed the wheel with her hands, then shook one after she hit it too hard. 'What now?'

Luke sighed and closed his eyes. They needed to get back, where were the bikes, he couldn't ride anyway, he needed sleep, his ribs hurt so much, he...

He couldn't think. He couldn't do anything. He was useless and pathetic and he wished he had a steering wheel to slam his fists against too.

'We need somewhere safe.'

He heard her as if from a distance. Then he heard the door slam and opened his eyes. The chair beside him was empty and he turned in his chair, hissing at the burst of pain. She was creeping across the road, away from the still-burning petrol station, sword out. He watched her, chest swelling again.

It wasn't like he'd done anything. A few days of training and a pep talk and he was acting like he was her dad. Although, he thought he'd be a better dad than the one she'd told him about. It wouldn't be difficult, but still, it was enough to make him smile.

Smoke drifted across the window, and when it dispersed she was out of sight. He gripped the sides of his chair and tried to take slow, shallow breaths. She'd be back in a moment, safe and sound.

He waited.

He was sweating, the chair behind his back hot and sticky. He longed to stand and walk around, but leaving the car was foolhardy. How long had she been gone? He knew it wasn't as long as it felt, but still... He twisted in his seat and stared in the direction in which she'd gone. Where was she?

He squirmed, sweating harder now. She'd been got. The bastard things had got her. The tears stung his eyes again and he scrubbed at them with his left hand. This was pathetic. This was what the Father had done to him. Maybe Seph and Az were right. Maybe it was time for a change.

A thump on the window made him gasp in relief and he turned to watch her clamber in. But the face that leered through the glass wasn't hers, and the yellow teeth that snapped shut again and again, made it quite clear what the zombie wanted. He shrunk in his seat, keeping as still as possible. It was pointless, of course. These things didn't hunt through motion or any such rubbish. It saw him as surely as he saw it and it knew he was fresh meat, untainted like the crap it'd probably been eating for the last week.

What would happen when all the humans were killed? Would the zombies eventually die out, or would they keep eating one another until only one was left, one monstrously fat zombie ruling the world? The thought would have been funny except the zombie outside was pretty fat and he was banging on the window, hands curled to display the horrendous claw-like fingernails adorning them.

Why was he so scared?

He was injured. He had seen plenty of sick and wounded humans and, for the most part, they'd displayed an admirable if sickening sense of spirit and determination. Until this point, he hadn't realised the courage they'd shown as well. But he was struggling to demonstrate anything except his ability to keep very still and pray for a sixteen year old girl to rescue him.

That *was* funny. Laughter burst out through his closed lips, making his stomach ache and driving pain through his chest and arms. The zombie banged harder, like it was an impatient customer at the drive-thru, greedy for burger and fries. He laughed harder, pain interspersing his laughter with whimpers.

The zombie was going to break the window. He stopped laughing. Suddenly it froze and slipped down the window. As the top of its head came into view, he saw the sword buried in it and sighed. He didn't care about the shame, she was back, and he was deeply and absurdly grateful.

She shoved the zombie out of the way and climbed in. 'Right, there's a house across the street. I can't see anything in there and the back door's open. We can get across to it pretty easy. I met one zombie on the way over, but the smoke's driving them away, so the time to go is now. You alright?'

He gave her a smile he knew was weak but hoped was convincing enough to reassure her. Either she didn't notice the weakness or chose not to, because she jumped straight back out of the car and came around to his side. The door opened and she grabbed him, helping him pull himself out. They stood together, Krystal putting her shoulder beneath his. She'd made it sound like a short dash but there were a couple of hundred yards and an impromptu car park between it and them. He took a deep breath. He had to make it, he had no choice.

They set off, him hobbling along, her doing everything she could to make it easier for him. She shoved him along, keeping the pace up, and he was more relieved than he thought possible he'd brought her along today. Anyone else and he'd have been dead twice over by now.

They weaved between the cars, slamming knees and hips into them at regular intervals. Slowly but surely the house grew closer and with it came more and more pain. Every step he took sent shocks rushing from his shoulder out across his body, urged on by his rib.

They were close to the pavement when the first zombie came. 'Stay standing,' she shouted it as she let him go. He put both hands out to balance himself and swayed side to side. Krystal leapt onto the bonnet of the nearest car, skipped across it and swung her sword like a golf club. It went straight through the zombie's face, splitting it in half and splattering pieces of nose and brains across the bonnet of a nice white Mini.

She hustled back to him and they moved on. By the time they reached the house he could no longer breathe, his chest hitching and stabbing over and over again. He hadn't imagined pain could be this intense but it wasn't stopping. His face and back were drenched in sweat, his socks damp in his shoes.

She dragged him around the back and in through the door of the kitchen. It was a tiny two-up two-down, which suited their needs just perfectly. She got him as far as the lounge and the two extraordinarily comfortable-looking sofas before she let him go. She disappeared for a moment and returned with a glass of water and a packet of aspirin. He downed four, lay back, and the blackness washed over him.

Dave

Ed was easy to talk to. The others always seemed confused around him, as though they expected something else. But Ed was happy to talk about games and movies and anything else that went through his mind. Dave couldn't remember much but each time Ed mentioned something he'd once known, it was like a tiny film in his head.

He thought they were memories maybe. Little slices of a life he neither remembered nor cared about. He knew it was a bad time and there had been something wrong with him. He knew more than that, because he knew how to eat and use the toilet and how to have a conversation and all sorts of things. He thought he could remember more, if he wanted to. He could lift the blanket that covered his memories and they'd all come spilling out.

But he didn't think it was a good idea. He didn't know why, he just knew the blanket should stay where it was. He had the vaguest sense that newer things were being pushed under there, too. But any time he searched for them, they slipped away. And he didn't care to look too hard.

So he chatted to Ed and his head began to fill with snapshots of games he'd played and movies he'd watched. He tried to care about it all like Ed clearly did, but he couldn't. There was nothing where the feelings should be. In the end, though, it didn't matter too much. Ed just wanted to talk and Dave was fine nodding at the right times and making the right encouraging noises.

He watched Bayleigh and Alex make their shabby attempts at getting Ed away from him. They thought he'd killed one of the ladies. He shook his head as he stared down at the street. He couldn't kill anyone, let alone a beautiful woman. Although, he still couldn't explain the rawness of his hands, like he'd been scrubbing them. And he couldn't remember where the scratches on his neck and arms came from either.

The answers were beneath the blanket. He paced across the room to the door. He paused before he opened it, holding his breath to listen. There was no one outside so he stepped out and strolled away down the hall. He would explore a bit more, try and find some corner of the hospital he had yet to document.

He was close to the edge of the field when Jackson burst out of the door before him and nearly knocked him down.

'Hi, Jackson, how are you?' It was one of those questions that meant nothing but he thought he should ask it. People seemed to expect it. The big man was panting and beads of sweat were running down his face. He was muttering to himself and Dave thought he wasn't going to respond.

Jackson raised his head. He looked surprised for a moment, before he squinted and stepped closer.

'Was it you?'

'I'm sorry?'

'Did you kill her?'

'I don't think so.'

'You don't think so? Either you did or you didn't. You don't get to be not sure about something like that.'

'There aren't many things I'm sure about. I'm sure about the number of stair wells in the hospital and the sleeping arrangements of every person in here. I'm not sure who killed the lady.'

Jackson's eyes narrowed further and his head cocked to one side. 'What are you saying? You think I did it?'

'No, not really. I don't think anyone did it. No, that's not correct. Someone did do it. I'm not sure who that someone was. That's better. Why, did you do it?'

Jackson growled, sneered at him, then shoved him aside and stomped away. Dave watched him go. That was... peculiar. Dave raised a hand in farewell and continued on his journey. He passed through the door and bumped into Bayleigh and Alex. 'Hi, guys, everything okay?'

They both gave him a funny look and Bayleigh stepped closer, lowering her voice. 'Have you seen Jackson?'

'Yes, he just... well, he accused me of something and then ran away. Why?'

Bayleigh took a deep breath. 'We think he killed the lady, Sian.'

'Sian?'

'The lady who died. Her name was Sian.'

'Oh.'

'Where are you going?'

'To explore, you know, the usual. Have you seen Ed? I was enjoying our conversation.'

They shook their heads and he knew they were lying. So they thought Jackson did it but still didn't trust him either. It would have hurt, had he cared either way. He had to admire their caution, even if not their detective skills. What had made them choose Jackson as the prime suspect? Except, of course, his psychopathic tendencies and scary manner. Looked at like that, they were probably right.

Dave strolled out into the hospital. He found a whole number of interesting things, including a great deal of drugs. He read the packets and pamphlets from beginning to end and left the pharmacy area knowing considerably more about the field of prescription medicine. He also took a few with him, things they might need were they to have to move suddenly.

The rest he left scattered across the floor. He found other things, too, but nothing as interesting, and once his feet started to hurt he made his way back to the ward. He should eat something. His appetite seemed to have gone the same way as his emotions, but he recognised the ache in his stomach as a physical need. So he ate something from the supplies, smiling easily at the women in the room.

They floated around like ghosts, silent and white-faced. Were they still shocked by the death of their comrade or was it his presence? He should find out. Not now, though. He settled himself in a corner with a sandwich and watched the ghosts. More and more came until the room was packed. They were making sandwiches, far more than they needed for an afternoon snack.

They were storing them away in bags and leaving the room in ones and two. Something was happening. He should probably care about it. He should tell Bayleigh and Alex so they could care about it. But he had his sandwich to finish. Soon the room was empty save for the two women that had been in here since he came in. With the rest of them leaving, those two brightened up and started chatting animatedly. He watched them, enjoying the quick smiles and eyes that flicked his way.

Something stirred, deep in his stomach, and his breathing sped up a little. They were enchanting.

He struggled to explain to himself what that word meant but it was the right one. They were casting a spell on him, lifting him up and away from himself.

He didn't know how long he sat there, but the light was different in the room when one finally stretched, making his breath catch in his throat, and wandered out. The other gave him a shy smile as she followed her friend. He returned it, pressing his hands flat against his legs.

A commotion stirred him from his chair and he strolled out into the corridor. The first thing he saw was Jackson, towering and strong at the far end of the corridor. Between them was a large group of ladies, maybe half of them. He saw amongst them the sandwich makers. Jackson clapped his hands.

'Everyone ready?'

Murmurs of assent filled the corridor and, with a final nod, he turned and set off out of the field. The ladies followed him, tromping down the corridor like they were heading for war. Jackson had almost reached the door when Bayleigh appeared. She was too far away for Dave to hear but he could guess what she was saying. Jackson was leaving! And he was taking a pretty decent number of the ladies with him.

That he hadn't asked Dave to go with him stung more than he expected. It shouldn't have stung at all, but there was something in his mind, a quiet voice that suggested Jackson should have asked him, that made it sting. He ignored it and focused on the exchange between the two of them.

Jackson was clearly disinterested, flapping his hands about before giving up and pushing past Bayleigh. Her words reached Dave now as she spoke to the women.

'Don't go with him, you don't know what you're doing. He murdered one of you, don't be so stupid.'

The ladies ignored her. Soon the corridor was empty save Bayleigh, who stood at the end, head hanging down. Dave sauntered towards her. 'They've all gone.'

She looked up and he was surprised to see how twisted and tired her face looked. 'Why?' She asked him. 'Why the hell would they go out there? All because of Luke? Can't they see what religion did to the people in St Paul's? It was religion that got them kidnapped and spellbound and they're still leaving because of it.'

She shook her head and hissed through her teeth and Dave realised she wasn't really talking to him. 'Why has Jackson gone?'

'You can't guess? It's just him now, him and forty something attractive young women. If he can't get his end away now, when will he be able to?'

'You think he's gone with them to have sex?'

Bayleigh burst out laughing. 'Who are you and what have you done with David? You're the guy who was cheating on his wife, you tell me.'

'I did what? Oh, I was, yes of course. Well, yes, but we didn't... I mean, I think we didn't love one another.' He frowned as the blanket twitched and pictures slipped out from underneath, people called Amber and Steph. The names were like branding irons cast into freezing water, the hiss and steam rising through his mind.

'So that made it okay to cheat?'

'I don't... I don't know. I can't believe Jackson would put everyone in jeopardy just for that.'

She gave him a level look and shrugged. 'I can. I also believe he'd do it just to piss us off. Maybe God told him to.'

She finished with a sneer and stalked past Dave. He turned and watched her. 'What now?'

She stopped and spun around, raising her hands and shoulders. 'I don't know. Why should I know, I've just screwed that up pretty successfully. We wait for Luke and Krystal and do our best to keep everyone safe from the zombies.'

She stomped off and he nodded at her back. She was probably right. He'd forgotten what he came out here to do so he went into the main room. There were a number of the ladies in here and Alex as well. He thought about talking to him but what did they have to talk about? Did Alex play games?

The lady who'd given him the smile was in here and as he walked in, she walked past and out of the door. She gave him another smile and he felt the same heat in his stomach. He turned and followed her out. She'd taken a few steps before she stopped.

He drew closer as she turned around. She blinked a bit and smiled again. 'Hi, I'm Tilda.'

'Dave.' He didn't have much else to say. The voice from beneath the blanket told him he'd never had that problem before. 'Where are you going?'

'I was just going to lie down and have a read. It's weird, I'm really tired and we aren't doing anything.'

'Inactivity can have a negative effect upon energy levels. It's always best to get some exercise in every day if you can.'

She blushed. 'What sort of exercise would you suggest?'

He was about to say brisk walking or swimming when he realised what she was asking. He blushed as well and grinned. 'All sorts. Anything that makes you sweat is good.'

He didn't know where the words came from but they seemed to work because she reached out and took his hand. 'Maybe you could show me some-thing that would make me sweat, help me get rid of this tiredness.'

He nodded mutely and let her lead him down the corridor. Something was changing in him, a mist that covered the blanket and everything else inside him. He felt hollow and that space was filled, just like that, with a fire that made him pant. As he followed her through the door, his mind went and the mist came down.

Bayleigh

She'd failed. She didn't know what she could have done differently, but still, she felt like a failure. Luke would return and she'd have to tell him everything that had happened. She'd have to explain about the murder, about Jackson and Harriet, and he'd look at her and she wouldn't know what to say.

Krystal, too. She was almost worse because Bayleigh knew she looked up to her. She'd have that look in her eyes of being let down. She shuddered and stormed past Dave. She couldn't bear talking to him. Anyone else and maybe it would have helped, but with him, all she wanted to do was shout until she elicited some kind of response. It was like talking to her father. He had this disconnect that meant all the parts of his brain weren't working properly.

He was still trying to excuse his cheating. Even since he'd changed, he still wanted to make out like it wasn't a bad thing to do. She sneered. Where was

Alex? Talking to Alex would help. Although, why hadn't he spoken up more when they met Jackson?

That had been a complete mess.

'Hi Jackson. Tell me, exactly, what you've been doing for the last two hours.' She asked.

'What?'

'I said—'

'I heard what you said. Why do you wanna know?'

He was on the defensive straight away. 'I'm just curious, that's all.'

'Yeah, well, shove your curiosity.'

He went to push past her and she put her hand on his chest. It was like putting her hand on a horse's flank. 'Someone's been murdered.'

To his credit, Jackson looked shocked. It lasted all of five seconds before he asked who. Was that a good sign or a bad one? He handled the news well but asked the most natural question someone who didn't know about it would ask. But then again, he was a dodgy bastard who had plenty of experience at lying to people.

'One of the ladies. A girl called Sian.'

'Zombies?'

'No. Someone pushed her eyes in so hard they went through to her brain. Someone who was strong and aggressive and could hold her down while he did it.'

'Any idea who it was?'

He was playing it very cool. She didn't know when she'd flipped from blaming Dave, but it was Jackson or no one at all. 'Actually, I was thinking it might be you.'

The moments the words left her mouth she knew they were the wrong ones. She could have talked around the subject, given him a chance to reveal himself. Instead she'd just barrelled in and now he was staring at her like she'd... well, accused him of murder. It was going to be difficult to explain why.

'You think it was me? Why is that I wonder? I'm black, so that doesn't help. And I'm big. It's easy to imagine me holding someone down, isn't it? How about my past life, that hanging over me too?' He looked from her to Alex, lips curled back. 'So which is it? Are you racist, or simple, or just unwilling to accept I've changed. I've done my penance—'

'No, you haven't. I don't know what you did in your 'past' life, but you've done no penance. You've just been lucky there aren't any police around to arrest you.'

'Isn't that a shame. My penance is internal and you got no idea what I've been through inside. How dare you accuse me—'

'Stop shouting. If it wasn't you, then who was it?'

'I don't bloody know, how the hell should I know? How big was the lady? Maybe there are other ones with the strength to do it. Maybe it was two of them. Maybe it was Dave, or Alex.'

He waved his hand past her and she glanced back at Alex. He shifted from foot to foot, but didn't try to deny it. And why should he? 'He was with me when it happened.'

'Oh yeah, he's been with you all day. Probably all night as well. Maybe if you weren't spending all your time shagging you'd have stopped it from happening.'

'What? Don't make this about us. Until you can convince me otherwise I think you murdered Sian and—'

'Yeah, you already said that. But unless you can convince me otherwise, I ain't staying here to be insulted.'

He shoved past her and stomped off down the corridor.

That had been a couple of hours ago. Then they'd left. She hadn't really believed it was going to happen until she stepped out into the corridor and watched them form up like they were going to war. Jackson had some of the devices. She didn't know how many, and when she grabbed him and asked, he refused to speak to her, waving her away.

She hadn't meant to shout at the ladies. But her self-control had gone the way of her exhaustion. There was nothing she could do and she knew it before she shouted, but she tried anyway. And then they walked away and she was left deflated and defeated. After her brief chat with Dave she was also pissed off. With a long sigh, she strode away down the corridor in search of Alex.

She found him with Sophie and paused in the doorway, watching them. Sophie was a simple soul, she'd decided. Not stupid, but she didn't seem to question anything. She was probably great in school, but in the big bad world Bayleigh could imagine her getting swallowed up. Watching her now, her big brown eyes turned up to Alex in a way that made her squirm, she knew she was close to the truth.

She turned her gaze his way. He was young, too young for her. She'd known it long before she started wondering about them, but she'd chosen to ignore it. Now she was regretting it. He had his easy smile on and he was smart. Probably too smart for her as well. She turned away and sniffed, letting out another long sigh. She wanted to sleep, but she couldn't. She'd grabbed two hours last night and that had been more than enough.

She could check the devices and see what Jackson had left them. The moment she thought about it, she flushed. How hadn't she done it already? Maybe Alex had. She shook her head. Not a chance, not while Sophie was there to give him her big smile and big eyes.

She grabbed a sandwich, forcing herself to eat as she strode to the first hiding spot. Ten minutes later she'd moved the other one she found to make sure the main rooms and surrounding bedrooms were covered. She moved Ed from their private room, which was now only half covered. They'd just got a bunch of bedrooms back, so they took one and Ed settled himself on one of the beds, reading happily.

She headed for reception, hoping for the best but expecting the worst. She couldn't decide how Ed was handling things. He was quiet and had spent most of the last five days in a book. He seemed happy with that. But his face was naturally sunny and his long hair hid any other expressions he may be making, so she just didn't know.

She found it easy to chat to Krystal. The girl had wanted to talk and told her all about her childhood, which was too horrible for Bayleigh to even contemplate. But Ed was young, and seemed even younger when compared to Krystal. She didn't even know how to start the conversation. How could you ask someone in the middle of the zombie apocalypse if they were happy?

She crept down the stairs, crouching to see the front door before she got too low. No zombies. Yet. She rushed the rest of the way and dashed around the reception desk. She hauled it open and swore as she stared into the empty drawer. He'd taken three of them. That absolute bastard had left them with only two devices and more than half the ladies. That the two upstairs were freshly charged mollified her only slightly.

She checked for the metal pole and found it tucked down one side. She lifted it, testing the weight like she knew what to do with it. She was tempted to wait for the zombies to start arriving. Hitting something was just what she needed right now. Needed was the right word. It wasn't just to let off steam, she needed to *do* something.

The spell had changed her. She was sleeping four out of every twenty four hours and eating maybe twice while she was awake. She'd lost weight but not so she looked bad. And she buzzed. It had almost faded into the background, but any time she focused on her body she felt it, like electricity running through her veins. She hadn't told the others, they'd only laugh at her complete inability to describe it.

But there was no better way to say it. She was different. But how different? Maybe she should find out. This was a good a time as any, and there was no one around to laugh if it went wrong.

She leant the pole back up and set herself, ready to run. When she set off, her eyes were fixed on the opposite wall of reception. It was maybe thirty metres away. She reached it in a couple of seconds and wasn't even breathing hard. She shook her head, turned around, and did the same on the way back. She grinned. She was fast. But then she already knew that. What else could she do?

She headed for the row of chairs sat against one wall. They weren't bolted down, so she grabbed the two in the centre, one arm beneath each, and heaved. They didn't move. She tried again and her back protested. No super strength then. She messed around, trying to move things with her mind or set fire to stuff in the same way, before concluding that speed was what she'd got.

How the hell had it happened? It all came from the spell the doctor did. It was magic, real magic. How did magic exist and everyone not know about it? She needed to ask Luke and get the info, though right now, the ability to break the 100 metres sprint record was a little more important. Not that anyone would know or care.

She chuckled. She was the fastest human on the planet. If only that was as impressive as it sounded.

This wasn't real. None of this was real. She could have handled just the zombies, or just Lucifer, but combine the two and add in some mysterious religious fanatics with magic and she was going crazy.

She wanted to run some more.

She was about to race off through the hospital when a zombie came in through the sliding doors. It lurched this way and that, its smart suit still in remarkably good condition. She loped to the desk, noting as she got there that the zombie had only taken one step.

She gripped the bar and stepped out to face it. This was it. She could do this. If Krystal could go all Lara Croft then so could she. And she wanted that sword. She hesitated another moment then ran around behind the zombie. It barely reacted, eyes still fixed on where she'd been standing. She slammed the metal pole over its head as hard as she could.

The skull gave way but the zombie stayed on its feet and swung around. She danced back out of reach, staying well clear of its hands. It attacked and she ran around it. It felt a little like doing PE at school, running around a post or something. She got another clear shot at its head and this time she brought the pole from right behind her head.

The skull caved in, the pole sinking deep into the softness beneath. The familiar smell of rot burst free and she gagged as she hauled her weapon free. The corpse dropped and she stepped back. That was more like it. She could do this. She'd keep the pole. With no device to keep them out, the zombies would be back in the hospital soon. Better to have their defences as near the field as possible.

With a grin, she turned away from the corpse and ran up the stairs. She took them three at a time and wasn't the least bit puffed out when she reached the top. For a few brief minutes, the troubles with Jackson and the ladies fled, and left her feeling light on her feet. But they came rushing back when she arrived in the field and heard the angry voices of the remaining ladies raised in argument.

She almost turned away. Almost. She set the pole against the door of the main room and stepped in.

Krystal

Luke was unconscious. She could handle that. She could handle all of this, easy. Trying hard to keep her hands and her breathing steady, she inspected the house. In each room, she made sure the windows were locked and the curtains drawn. It was like making a squat.

She only done one squat. She'd lasted a couple of weeks before the guys she went in with decided they had their own little kingdom and suggested she owed them. She hadn't liked the smell either. There was something about living in a building that wasn't a home anymore that made people disrespect it. At least the hostels were cleaned. Outside was even better, so long as the sun was shining.

They weren't hiding from the police here, though. She never thought she'd wish it was the police but that would have been so much better. Anything would have been better that zombies. The downstairs was secure and she tiptoed up. She wasn't expecting anything but it paid to be cautious. It always paid to be cautious.

There were three bedrooms up here and the first contained a double bed and clothes scattered on a chair. She drew the curtains and glanced down into the back garden. It was still empty but in the garden beyond there were two zombies. They had bats in their hands and stood idle either side of a Swingball post. The tennis ball hung on its string as both zombies feebly batted at nothing. It brought a lump to her throat so she closed the curtains completely.

The next bedroom was tiny and contained a cot and a chest of drawers. She drew the curtains and turned back to the cot. The lump in her throat was replaced with sick so she scrambled into the bathroom and spat it into the sink. She gripped the porcelain with both hands, staring at her distorted reflection in the taps.

She'd imagined it. There was no way, there was just no way.

She had to check.

She couldn't go back in there.

She let go of the sink and stared at her hands. They shook, trembling like she was ninety years old and suffering from drink, and she wasn't surprised. She swallowed, tasted sick and spat again. She washed her mouth out and swilled the sick away. Then she began to clean the sink with pieces of toilet roll. Anything to avoid what she knew she had to do. Finally she dumped the toilet roll in the loo and stepped into the hallway.

She waited outside the room, hoping Luke would wake and call her, or a zombie would attack downstairs.

She was actually hoping a zombie would attack.

Her forehead creased and she stepped back into the baby's room. It lay in the cot, a tiny bundle with greying skin and deep sunk eyes. As she looked down into the cot, it opened its mouth, showing red raw gums. That was the final straw and she couldn't stop the tears from welling up.

Did zombies grow up? Would it get bigger and bigger until it could climb out the cot? Or was it doomed to be that age forever, lying here until whatever reserves it had left ran out? That begged another question, one that drew her mind blessedly away from the truth of what she had to do. What happened if zombies didn't eat?

They had formed packs and were hunting, running down the slower and weaker zombies and feasting on them. But what would happen to a baby like this? It had lain here for six days and was still alive, so how long would it last? She wanted the answer to be that it would soon be done and she could leave it. But she wasn't convinced. If it had gone this long, who was to say it wouldn't still be wriggling in another six days?

She turned back to the cot and the pathetic thing inside it. This was Etienne's fault. His and the demon and angel Luke had called his friends. They had done this and she wanted nothing more than to find them and kill them. Not just for this, but for making her do what she had to now.

She drew her sword and raised it above the cot. She couldn't watch so she lined the tip up with the baby's head and squeezed her eyes closed. She shoved as hard as she could and barely felt it as the blade went through. She yanked it out and wanted nothing more than to run from the room, but she had to be sure.

The baby's eyes were closed, the front of its forehead caved in. Krystal staggered from the room. She made it into the third bedroom before she collapsed completely. She thought she'd forgotten how to cry, then the thing with Ed had taught her how all over again. Now she sobbed, huge racking bursts that she thought would never finish and made her whole body ache.

They did end, eventually, once she was too tired and her eyes had dried up. She checked all the doors again and laid down. Despite the afternoon sun coming in the windows, she was soon asleep.

The night woke her with a chorus of moans and groans and growls. She sat with a jolt, from sleeping to wide awake in moments, and held her breath. The sound was all around and made her shiver and hug herself. What the hell was going on?

She knew where she was and she knew Luke was passed out on the sofa downstairs. She also knew she had the most horrendous headache. And she knew there was a baby with a hole in its head in the cot in the next bedroom. She glanced at the door as though the sad little creature was going to come crawling through on all fours.

The groaning sounded like an army of the dead just outside. But the zombies weren't an army. She clambered off the bed and sneaked to the window, hands reluctantly reaching for the curtains. She twitched them aside and peeked out. The dark of the night was disturbed by rows of street lamps. Even with everyone dead there was still too much light to see the stars.

But she wasn't looking for stars. She stared into the front lawn where a horde of zombies pressed themselves against the windows and front door. Their arms were raised and she saw the clawed hands, made yellow by the lights, thumping and banging against the windows.

She scampered through to the back bedroom, wiping the sweat off her forehead, and peered out. The story in the back was the same, a row of zombies two deep pushing at the house as though they could knock it over. She clapped her hand over her mouth before she could scream. She didn't want to wake Luke. They were safe in here. But how had they found them? How the hell did they even know there was anyone in here for them to eat?

She was about to close the curtains when she heard a different growl, louder and higher-pitched than the others. As one, the zombies stopped and turned. From out of the group came one dressed in a mini skirt and leather jacket. She had her hands above her head but as soon as she stood alone on the lawn, she pointed at the side gate.

The zombies broke away from the house and Krystal ran into the side bedroom. The window was smaller here and she had to press her face up against it to avoid the glare. The zombies charged from the side gate and she spotted their target only seconds before they reached him. A lone zombie weaved side to side down the pavement outside. They hit him like a rugby tackle and how he was still in one piece as they dragged him back through the gate was a mystery.

She swapped bedrooms as they brought their prey back into the garden. They dumped him at the feet of the women zombie in the miniskirt and set up another round of growls. The woman put her foot on the zombie's face and grabbed his arm. Then, to the increasingly loud shouts of the crowd, she twisted it until it ripped from its socket. She brought it to her mouth and took a huge bite, then raised the arm above her head as blood streamed from her teeth.

The crowd growled in appreciation and fell on the zombie, tearing it apart. The woman set to work on the arm, tearing chunks of rotting flesh out with her teeth.

Krystal watched because she couldn't look away.

There was nothing she wanted more but she couldn't. They were getting smart, learning things, following others. Alex had said they couldn't, that their brains wouldn't work like that, but they were. And she was leading them. There was a, what was the word Luke used? A hierarchy.

She closed the curtains and sat on the bed. They were trapped in a house by a pack. She'd brought them here and they were trapped. She dashed down the stairs into the lounge and gasped. The sofa was empty. She raced through to the kitchen and let out a long breath.

Luke was by the window, the blinds pulled slightly apart.

'Morning.'

'No, it's not, it's the middle of the bloody night. You should be lying down.'

He turned and grinned at her. 'You're as bad as Bayleigh.'

'How's your shoulder.'

He rolled it slowly and grimaced at the movement. 'Not great. Certainly not going away. But then,' he waved at the window, 'it doesn't look like we're going anywhere anyway.'

'Did you see it all?'

'I didn't see them take the guy out but I can imagine it. They're learning.'

She snapped her fingers together. 'That's just what I thought. It's horrible.'

'Yes it is. I think we're safe in here, but we can't have both of us sleeping again. I'm feeling quite awake if you want to lie down?'

She barked a laugh. Like sleep was ever going to come with that noise outside the windows.

Krystal spent the rest of the night sat on the edge of the sofa, jumping every time the groaning grew louder. The feeding occurred twice more before the sun came up, the zombie leader making a sort of growling scream that made her skin crawl the same way it had when certain business men smiled at her. Why was that one stronger than the rest? Why was it smarter?

They wouldn't ever know. She and Luke discussed it in hushed tones. Talking loudly, despite the creatures already knowing they were here, just seemed wrong. The conclusion they reached was that they would never know. They also decided it didn't matter. There was nothing they could do to stop it or change it, so why worry?

She was surprised at how easy it was to accept. It was like her mind had created a switch. Once she'd stabbed a baby through the head, there weren't many things that were going to trouble her.

They also decided they needed guns. The swords were great for a tight spot, but not having something more powerful was daft. So on the way home they were going to stop outside Buckingham palace and try and get some guns. There was no talk of not making it home and she was grateful. In her heart of hearts, she didn't think they were ever leaving this house, but Luke didn't seem to get the idea of doubt.

The sky was lightening when she drifted off again, head lolling side to side on the back of the sofa.

She didn't know what woke her the next time, but she was bathed in sweat and curled up tight on the cushions. A nightmare perhaps, a sleeping one this time. Her eyes drifted slowly closed then opened wide as she saw Luke, slumped in the chair opposite. His eyes were closed and his chest moved in the slow steady breaths of sleep.

She sat up, blinking and rubbing her eyes.

Then she heard it. She knew what it was straight away, despite wishing it was anything else. She peeled herself from the sofa and trudged into the kitchen, hands gripping her trousers.

She pressed her knuckles against her teeth and tried not to scream. She watched with her chest tightening as the handle on the back door moved slowly down. Weight came against the door and pushed. It was locked, of course, but they tried again and again. Still she was frozen, watching blankly as her mind ran in circles.

Finally the handle stopped moving and she waited. Nothing. She crept closer and listened, holding her breath. Nothing. She let out a long sigh, turned and jumped as something hit the lounge window. The crack that followed forced a scream from her. As she dashed out of the kitchen, another thing hit the window and it shattered, scattering shards of glass across the floor.

Part Two

Jackson

He stepped out and smelled the air. The familiar tang of London was blemished by the rot. He hadn't noticed it in the hospital, but out here the smell was everywhere. It was food and vegetables, going off in the shops. It was bags of rubbish that would never be collected. It was the bodies, or what was left of them, once the packs had been through. Everything was rotting.

He blinked and glanced behind him. The glass reflected his face and he stared at it. He was thinner and leaner. More wolf than bear now. The way the Lord wanted it. Harriet said he was God's chosen. She'd said it almost the minute they left the hospital and his chest had swelled as he walked before them down to the river. He felt like a XXX version of the pied piper, leading his women to a new world.

He turned away and the memories fled. That had been three days ago and the feelings were quite different now. He was alone. High above him, in the tip of the Shard, his ladies spent their time chatting and reading and doing each other's hair. He spent it sitting in his own room, alternating between masturbation and self-flagellation. His feelings were sinful. He recognised them now, not as the normal urgings of a man for a woman, or women, but as the desperate cravings for something beyond him.

He was God's chosen and that meant a life dedicated to the Lord. Everything given up for the Lord. He sniffed and thumbed his nose. He stomped down to the river and stood beside the HMS Belfast looking across at Tower Bridge. This wasn't why he left. God had sent him here to keep them safe, but they were too safe. Their device kept the zombies at the bottom of the stairs and even when it ran out he would fill the stairwell with furniture and bolt the doors and they could live there for a very long time.

There was a garden just along from where he stood and they were looking at it as a place to grow food. He spat into the river and watched it float atop the brown water. What was he doing? Why was he here? He wasn't killing zombies, that was for sure. He wasn't doing anything to end the plague or bring life back to the Earth.

He knew where the frustration came from. He knew it but however hard he beat himself and however many times he drove the nails through his arms, still he couldn't get rid of it. If he could just have one of them. It didn't even have to be Harriet. She made his dick hard just thinking about her, and she would bear him sons, he knew it, but any of them would do. He growled and spun away from the river. There were zombies on the Belfast, lurching along the side. He pulled his gun from his waistband and leant against the rail.

He took careful aim, shot, and smiled as a zombie tumbled into the river. He shifted slightly, shot again, and another went down. This one crumpled against the wall behind it and other zombies closed in, biting into the dead flesh. Jackson turned away from the river and made his slow way back to the Shard.

Where was he? Who was he? He paused before the glass and stared at himself. He was a better person now, he knew that, but at least before his rebirth he'd known who he was and what he was doing. The pursuit of money wasn't evil or wrong. Now he knew nothing except the frustration in his trousers and the ever-strengthening belief he should be doing something else.

And where was Az? The bastard had promised to send soldiers but he was nowhere and no soldiers had arrived. He hissed and pushed through the door. The zombies in the lobby growled but were pushed back by the field as he headed for the lift. Minutes later he stepped out into the hotel.

The Shard had been an excellent idea. The top few floors were a hotel, and a nice one at that. They'd spread out and were living in luxury. There were kitchens up here and the electricity was still on so the fridges were stocked full. Apparently the electricity could go off at any moment, but he would enjoy it while it lasted.

They'd seen an explosion in their first day here, down south way. Something big went up and there was a plume of black smoke for a good few hours. A couple of the ladies who seemed to be thinking about this stuff said it would happen more and more as equipment wasn't maintained and pipes got corroded. The Shard was brand new, though, so it should take longer to corrode. That's what he told himself anyway. Right now, he didn't care all that much.

And that was sinful. His life was a gift and not caring about it, even for a second, was the worst thing he could do. He stomped for his room, determined that this time he would beat the thoughts from himself. He was halfway down the corridor when another door opened and Harriet's head poked out.

'Jackson, where have you been?'

He almost snapped at her, but the part of him that refused to believe he wouldn't ever have her, stopped him. 'Went down to the river, get some air.'

'Well, come in here.'

She waved him in and he swallowed. She spoke to him like he was some leader or other and he liked that plenty, but she'd never invited him into her room. He walked in and stopped. She was wearing a blouse and panties and nothing else. She waved at the chair, then sat herself on the bed, knees drawn up to her chest with her arms across them. Every time she shifted he caught sight of her pussy pressed against the white cotton of her panties.

'I need to talk to you. But first, I think there's something else we need to do.'

She rose from the bed and began undoing her blouse. He tried to speak, to explain that his life was given to God. But all that came out was a low growl. When he picked her up and threw her on the bed, all she gave him in reply was a look that made him even harder. Her panties snapped as he tried to haul them off and she didn't care.

She groaned when he entered her, struggling to contain him, but she got wet soon enough. For the first time in two weeks, Jackson forgot all about God.

When they were finished, she pushed him off and sat up. 'Okay, can we talk properly now?'

He lay back on the pillow, one arm over his head. 'How about we do some more of that?'

'Once is more than enough, thank you. You've been good for nothing since we got here and I understand why. I know about men's urges and I don't blame you for them. But now we're done I expect you to get focused.'

The tone of her voice, so businesslike and matter of fact, made him blink a few times. He watched her walk naked across to the bathroom. She was so fine. And she was getting in the shower. He grinned and climbed out of the bed. The water was running when he climbed in behind her and put his hands on her tits. She jumped and stiffened against him and he waited for the inevitable softening.

She turned within his arms and their eyes met. He almost took his arms away, but didn't. Then he felt her hand on his dick and grinned. She gripped him hard and his grin widened. Harder still and the smile slipped. She brought her lips close to his ear, water flicking off them as she spoke. 'I'm going to keep squeezing until I break your penis. I don't know what will happen when it goes, but I'm guessing going to the toilet will hurt like nothing else.'

His arms dropped. Who was she to talk to him like this? Who the hell did she think she was? He grabbed her round the throat and slammed her against the wall of the shower. Her hold on his dick loosened and she tried to speak, but her face was already going pink as he choked the life from her. Stupid, greedy, teasing bitch, who the hell did—.

He let go and she struck the floor of the shower, sliding down until she lay halfway between his legs. Her face was near his dick but it was soft and getting softer. The water hammered down and stole the first tears that came from his eyes. Then he threw himself out of the shower and into the bathroom, slipping to his knees for a moment.

He staggered into her room and fell again, driving his face into the ground between his legs as though he could scare away his sin. He was evil. He thought he'd beaten it, but it was still in him, still strong. He howled, the sound muffled by the floor but the pain no less real.

The shower switched off. He heard her enter the bedroom, the gentle pad of her naked feet across the carpet. She was still naked and he couldn't help the stirring between his legs. How could he? How could he apologise? Nothing he could say would make this any better.

Her footsteps changed. She had boots on now and he waited for the door to open. Instead something struck him in the side, high up in the ribs. He grunted and rocked sideways, but stayed right where he was. Another blow in the same place and the pain was multiplied. With the third blow he thought his rib broke. He struggled to breathe and panted, his breath hot against his legs.

She moved on, driving the toe of her boot into his arse a few times until he whimpered. Then she slammed the heel down into his back. He was being punished. He deserved the punishment. This was what God wanted. This would drive the sin away. He could punish himself all he wanted but Harriet was one of God's ladies, one of his chosen, and she had the right to punish him.

The kicking stopped and he gasped, blackness closing in around the corners of his eyes. Then something else struck him and he hissed between his teeth. It was, he realised, the telephone from the side of the bed. It beat around his back and didn't hurt nearly enough, but when she started smashing him over the head and in the ears and side of the face, it hurt plenty.

He tried to hide, so she went around behind him and drove her boot between his legs. He was certain one of his balls burst and he screamed, shunting forward on the carpet to escape. She kicked him again and then went crazy with the phone, hitting him over and over again until he fell from his scrunched up position onto his side and covered his face with his hands.

Eventually the beating stopped. He cracked open his eyes and looked up. She stood above him, wearing nothing but her boots and a face full of tears. He wanted to say he was sorry, to beg forgiveness in the eyes of the Lord. But why should she forgive him?

'You can fuck me now.'

He blinked, not believing what he was hearing. But his dick was hard between his legs and despite the pain that racked his body he wanted nothing more than to lose himself in her. Her chest was heaving, her breasts thrusting out towards him, and this time she welcomed him as he grabbed her and shoved her against the wall.

Alex

Alex was itchy. He still clung to the secret he'd spent the last week guarding, expecting Luke to expose him at any moment. Except he hadn't, and the guilt had built and built until he was ready to scream.

He wasn't screaming though. He was sitting in the main room with Sophie, a beautiful woman his own age who was both deliciously naive and experienced. Not in that way, he was pretty certain, but there was more to her than she was letting on. There had to be, no one was this innocent.

Why couldn't he forget about his part in the plague and move on? No one else cared where it came from. The truth was, it came from the soldiers of God. If they hadn't stolen it from the government it would still be locked in a bunker deep below ground. So it was their fault. Him designing it made him no more guilty than the person who made the trucks in which it was delivered.

He nodded and Sophie stopped mid-sentence. 'You really think he was right?'

'What? Sorry, no, I...' He blushed and sat straighter. 'Sorry, I drifted off. There's a lot going on. What were you saying?'

She didn't even look affronted, just nodded and smiled and started again. He tried to pay attention this time, he really did, but it was difficult. Because regardless of who was to blame for the plague, he still couldn't deny the other problem that was growing larger by the minute. That problem sat across the room, hair tied back, attacking a sandwich and very pointedly not looking at him.

Did Bayleigh like him? He thought she did, but she was being very cool about it if she did. And she thought the age difference was an issue. She looked good, great for thirty four, but she'd nearly fainted when he said he was twenty two. Nearly fainted and then looked really disappointed. He blinked and focused on what Sophie was saying.

They'd moved onto her course at Uni and how thrilling it was and he realised he was in completely the wrong place talking to the wrong person. He excused himself and left the room, expecting to find Bayleigh wandering the corridors. They were deserted. It felt quiet in here since half the ladies had left. There were still fifty something of them crammed into a tiny space, but it was subdued, as though Jackson had dragged off all the ones with any spirit.

He headed for their room and found it empty, then went room by room through their area. After walking in on a couple of the ladies in fewer clothes than expected, he took to knocking on doors. He paused by one, hand raised, and stopped before he knocked. There were sounds coming from within and, face flushed, he leant closer.

They were... odd. There was a man in there who could only be Dave and he sounded like he was having a great time. But there was another voice that sounded strained and he couldn't decide if she was enjoying herself or not. Then her voice grew louder and broke as she said 'no' and Alex slammed the door open.

Dave was half naked, trousers around his ankles as he stood at the end of the bed. The woman lying in front of him was fully clothed. Her face was red and she was batting feebly at Dave's hands where they latched around her throat.

'Dave, stop it, you're killing her.'

Dave turned to stare at him and Alex froze, one hand stretched out towards him. He was snarling, lips pulled back from his teeth like a dog, and his features were twisted in a way he could only describe as inhuman. There was something inside him, pushing at his skin as it tried to get out. Alex's stomach turned. It wasn't Dave he was looking at, but whatever was wearing his skin. And its hands were still tight around her neck.

Alex charged in and grabbed his arms. Dave retaliated by taking one hand away and backhanding Alex across the face. It was like being hit by a car and he flew back, slamming his back against the edge of the open door. He shouted in pain as he hit the floor, his hand twisting awkwardly beneath his body. Dave ignored him, hands once again around her neck.

Alex clambered up the door frame and searched for a weapon. The woman wasn't moving, her hands barely clawing at Dave's arms. Shit, shit, shit. He grabbed one of the tacky swivel chairs and hefted it off the floor. His first blow was clumsy, bouncing off Dave's shoulder and barely making him move. With the second swing he got Dave in the face and he released the woman, staggering back with his hands up.

Alex put himself between them, raising the chair in defence. Dave made a sound, like car tires squealing on tarmac, then rushed Alex with eyes that burned red. He almost dumped the chair and ran, but the woman on the bed was coughing which meant she was alive. He wasn't going to give Dave a chance to change that.

Dave ran straight into the chair and bashed Alex back against the bed. Then he grabbed the base of it and yanked it from Alex's hand. His heart sunk like he'd just stepped into traffic. Dave lunged and grabbed him by the face, fingers digging into his skin. He aimed a punch for Dave's face and got him on the chin. His head snapped back but his fingers dug further into Alex's cheek.

He made a sound deep in his throat as his eyes began to water. Dave was going to tear his face open. He found the bar that ran under the bed with one foot and pushed himself up until he stood a full head above Dave. The pressure on his cheek got worse until he was sure his skin was tearing. Then he threw himself on top of him. They went down in a shower of limbs and Dave's head cracked against the floor.

Dave went limp. Alex rolled off and lay on his back, sucking in air and staring up at the ceiling. The lady's face appeared over the edge of the bed. She looked first at Alex, who gave her a weak smile she didn't even attempt to return. Then she looked at Dave. Her expression grew grim and she scooted sideways off the bed.

She came around the end, arms wrapped around herself, and nudged him with her foot. He blinked and looked around. He caught sight of the woman and blushed, looked down at his naked legs and rumpled trousers and blushed even more.

'Did we... What am I doing on the floor?'

The woman stared at him and burst into tears. She booted him, but her heart wasn't in it. Alex scrambled to his feet and put his arm around her shoulders, hustling her out of the room. The moment they got into the corridor she extricated herself from his embrace and stood away from him. Her shoulders were heaving up and down and the tears were getting worse.

'Look, I think you should be with your friends, come on.'

He led her down the hallway to the main room and pushed through the door. The moment the women saw her they flocked and he pulled himself free of the mess. He trudged back to the room, trying to figure out what the hell happened next.

Dave had pulled his trousers up and was sitting on the bed, staring at his hands. He glanced up then back at his hands. 'What did I do?'

'You know you did something?'

'She was crying. And that look...' he trailed off. 'We came in here to have fun. You don't look at someone like that after you've shagged.'

'You didn't shag.'

'I figured that much out.'

His voice was still monotone, only rising slightly towards the end of his sentence. It was as though he was trying to pretend an emotion that wasn't there. Alex put his hands on his hips and stared at him. 'Do you honestly not remember what you just did?'

Dave shook his head, looking entirely calm. 'Nope, not a clue.'

'You strangled her. If I hadn't come in when I did, she'd be dead.'

Dave nodded. 'That's bad.'

'Yeah, just a bit. What happened?'

'I don't remember. She approached me and was flirting really heavy so I just went along with it. We came in here and then...' He shrugged and raised his hands. 'No idea.'

Alex paced back and forth across the room. 'I'm not sure they're going to believe that.'

'So?'

'Are you aware of what's just happened? Half of them have left, just buggered off to who knows where. The ones that are left need to feel safe and you've just strangled one half to death. That's not a good start.'

He didn't mention the murder. He'd discuss it with Bayleigh because he was now sure it was Dave. But what was to be gained? Should they lock him up somewhere? Why? What was the point? What did justice look like in the new world? He had a horrible feeling it wouldn't look like a nice jail cell and reha-bilitation. It was more likely to involve something a little more old-fashioned.

What bugged him was not knowing whether he was protecting Dave for Luke's sake or because he truly believed that getting him in a room and letting everyone attack him wasn't going to help. He'd never thought much about his morals, but with eve-rything that had happened, they felt paper thin and irrelevant.

He stopped pacing and looked at Dave. 'Why did you do it?'

'I don't know. I didn't know I was doing it.'

'So no motive. That makes you the best killer, you know?'

'I don't want to kill anyone.'

'Can I suggest avoiding one to one contact with anyone in the next, oh, seventy years or so then?'

'Why did it happen? What's wrong with me?'

'What happened in St Paul's? You buggered off and left Krystal on her own and when you came back you were different.'

He watched Dave's face carefully and saw the tell-tale signs. He was lying when he answered.

'Nothing. I mean, nothing I know about.'

His upturned eyes, so guileless, so lacking in any emotion, nearly sold it. But not quite. What had he done in St Paul's? And how the hell was he and Bay supposed to figure it out? He was back with the same problem again. How could he get the truth from him? Torture? He almost smiled, only it wasn't funny.

'C'mon, Dave, what happened?'

'Nothing. I mean it, I don't even remember what happened. I was so scared about getting down from the dome I just don't remember anything until I saw everyone coming through the cavern.'

Alex hissed and turned away. He cracked the door and put his ear to the gap. There were angry

voices again and he took a deep breath. By the time
Luke got back there'd be no one here. He pushed
through the door and paused.

'Stay here. Don't leave and don't come out. Do
you understand?'

Dave nodded, no less bothered by Alex's com-
manding tones than he had by the accusation earlier. Alex wandered slowly down the corridor and
paused when he saw Bayleigh come around the
corner. He almost shouted for her to stop, but he
wasn't sure he wanted to see her alone yet. He
didn't know what he was going to say.

So he waited and let her go in to the main room
first, then walked to the door and paused. And listened.

Luke

Something was broken. It could be his rib but he thought there was something else as well, something that had woken him. He'd been enjoying sleep, dreaming of Sara and a time when he didn't have to worry about being woken up, because he never really slept. He'd been good at pretending, lying down and closing his eyes and drifting. Many of them did it. It was another way to feel a little more human, a little more real.

But this was real sleep, when he lost himself entirely and the world went away. And now he was awake. Krystal screamed horribly near his ear and the remnants of sleep fled as he sat up. His chest burned and he doubled straight over, waiting for it to ease. It did, a little, enough for him to stand and turn. Krystal stood with her sword in hand, facing the curtains.

The wind was blowing them, which meant they were open. Why had she opened the windows? The stupidity of that thought brought him fully awake just as the curtains parted and the first zombie tumbled into the room. It actually fell, climbing over the window sill and toppling head first to the carpet. It would have been funny had he not caught a glimpse of what lay outside.

He nodded as Krystal thrust her sword straight through the back of its head and withdrew it just as quickly. One down. He shook himself, scooped his sword off the floor and drew it, dumping the scabbard on the sofa. The next one came through the same way and Krystal chopped the top of its head off before it had a chance to fall on the floor.

Luke joined her, stabbing the next one through the face as it appeared. 'What happened to the window?'

'They broke it. They threw something at it and broke it.'

He saw the fear on her face and couldn't disagree with it. They were learning.

'And there's a leader, some woman telling them what to do.'

'A zombie?'

'Of course a bloody zombie.'

He didn't have a chance to reply because three of them came through the window at the same time. One toppled onto the floor but he focused on one that swung its leg over the sill. He drove his sword straight down through its forehead and grinned as its face split apart. An eyeball fell into the gap and onto the floor.

Krystal dealt with the third and they turned together to the one on the floor. It stiffened as they hit it at the same time, destroying its face in the bargain. The window was empty for a moment and he took a deep breath.

'They're learning, but they aren't exactly smart.'

'That's not making me feel any better. How's your shoulder?'

He rolled it and winced. 'I'm trying to ignore it right now. Lucky I can fight with my left.'

'Oh yeah. That's a good trick.'

He flashed her a grin and stepped closer to the window. The curtain pushed in and another zombie appeared in the gap. He felt his shoulder this time, despite thrusting with the other hand, and the bite of the blade was inordinately satisfying. They could do this all night, there was nothing to worry about.

'Did you hear that?' She asked.

'What?'

'Listen.'

He stepped away from the window and heard it. A crack like a stone hitting glass. Suddenly there was a cascade of cracks and he heard one window shatter followed by another.

'Shit, we need a new plan.' Krystal backed away from the window, glancing over her shoulder. He nodded and ran past her, waving for her to follow. They ran into the tiny hallway between the lounge and the dining room and saw through the doorway the front window smashed and zombies already appearing in the gap.

He shoved Krystal up the stairs and raced after her until they reached the square of landing at the top. He was about to dive into the smallest room when Krystal stopped him.

'Don't go in there.'

He raised his eyebrows and she shook her head. She paled and kept shaking it. He shrugged and raced into another. Through the curtains he saw the crowds of zombies gathered around three windows downstairs. They were coming in faster now they weren't there to stop them.

'There.'

Krystal pointed to a zombie stood on the garden table pointing at the house. She looked like an extra in a bad B movie, exhorting her troops with huge waves of her arms.

'Can't you do anything to her?'

'Like what?'

'I don't know. What about your scary thing, you know, 'greatest fear' thing?'

Her impression of him was just close enough to make him smile. Then he heard feet on the stairs and ran out to the landing. They were coming, climbing the stairs on hands and knees. Ignoring Krystal's squeak of protest he headed into the smallest bedroom and saw the cot. He knew instinctively what he'd find in there, but he didn't need to look in it. He just needed to use it.

He slammed it into the door frame as he dragged it out. He lined it up with the stairs and shoved as hard as he could. Krystal groaned and he turned away, not wanting to see what fell out of it. What mattered was the thumps and growls as the zombie nearest them was driven back down the stairs.

The cot was lodged at the bottom of the stairs, dug into the wall on one side. He'd bought them a little time, but already one of the zombies was attempting to climb over it. Krystal was still pale, pointing down the stairs with a shaking finger.

'There was...'

'It doesn't matter. It was a zombie. They're all zombies. There's no cure.'

'Are you sure?'

He hesitated. He and Alex had pretended they could find one but the creatures they were killing didn't have a disease. They were a disease and their bodies were far beyond saving. There was no going back for them. He clenched his jaw and nodded. 'There's no cure. Their brains are gone.'

'So how come they're learning?'

She was far too sharp. 'I don't know. It's bizarre and illogical and very annoying.'

'Annoying. Not scary or horrible, just annoying?'

He flashed her a smile and checked down the stairs. The zombie was still struggling to get over the cot.

'How are we getting out of here?'

'You're just full of questions. How do you think we should get out of here?' He felt bad as soon as he snapped at her, but it was too late to take it back. Besides, four hundred years ago he'd have been willing the zombies to win, so maybe he shouldn't feel so bad.

He shook his head. That didn't work. It should have worked but it didn't and he felt just as bad. He had so much to blame the Father for, though he wasn't sure blame was the right word anymore. He needed more things to hit. He should apologise.

'We could get out on the roof.' Krystal interrupted his thoughts.

'And that would help how?'

'I don't know. But we aren't going out the front door.'

'Are you sure? Where are the bikes?'

'Up by the petrol station.'

'How far is it?'

'Five minutes maybe, if we run. Can you run?'

He grunted and nodded. He could run. His rib was feeling better. Maybe he'd just needed to move around and get it back in place. His powers here included a certain degree of unnatural healing, because there was no way his shoulder should be this much better.

'So maybe we do go out the front door.' He said.

'How? And, can I just say, you're mad and stupid.'

'You may. I'll save it for later when I need to remind you about the wisdom of climbing on to the
roof of St Paul's.' She dug him in the ribs and he
grinned. 'We're going to burn the place down. The
zombies won't like that and we can get out while
they panic.'

'I don't think zombies panic. And didn't Bayleigh
try this with the shop?'

Luke frowned. She had and he'd laughed at her
at the time. But he didn't have anything better, and
neither did Krystal.

'Only one way to find out.' He headed into the
main room, yanked the sheets off the bed, and piled
them up atop the mattress. He pulled his ruck sack
off his back and dug out the lighter. It took a minute
or two to get the sheets burning properly but soon
the bedroom was filling with smoke. Krystal burst
out coughing and he pulled her out to the landing.

'Keep low. It all rises, just stay on the floor.'

She crouched on all fours, facing down the stairs
to the zombie that had mounted the cot.

'You can deal with him while I light the other
room.' She scrambled down the stairs while he went
into the second bedroom and repeated the process.
Smoke was billowing out into the hallway when he
emerged. Krystal was sat on the stairs, the zombie
absent from the cot. There were more the other
side, but they had seen the smoke and no longer
seemed desperate to get upstairs.

Luke joined her, squeezed together above the cot, and put his hand on her shoulder. 'Ready?'

'Course not. What's the plan?'

'We kick the cot down the stairs, run past them and out the front door, get to the bikes and get away.'

'My helmet's in the lounge.'

'We'll find you another one. Let's go.'

He slammed his booted foot into the cot, and it stayed right where it was. It just needed a few more kicks. He tried again and again but the cot was being driven deeper into the plaster on the side of the stairs.

'Luke, is this gonna work?'

He glanced behind them as flames lashed out of the bedrooms to blacken the ceiling. The smoke was making its way down the stairs and he could feel the heat. 'Cover your face.'

'With what?'

'Your t-shirt maybe?'

'I'm not taking my t-shirt off in front of them.'

'Really?'

He gave her a look and she shook her head, lips pressed obstinately together. Then she coughed and glared at him. She settled for pulling her t-shirt up over her nose, exposing her skinny stomach. He followed suit and returned to kicking the cot. It was still stuck in the wall but the rail at his end finally cracked and broke in. He grabbed the side rails,

yanked them inwards, and the cot collapsed on itself.

Heaving a sigh of relief, he twisted it out of the
wall and threw it at the zombies. His eyes watered
and he had to blink furiously to clear them. Krystal
was still coughing, a steady hacking that had her
half-sitting on the steps, one hand pressed against
the wall.

The flames were licking down the stairs and the
carpet was on fire. Sweat coated the back of his neck
and he shifted his sword from one sweaty hand to
another.

'Come on, it's now or never.'

Krystal nodded and tried to rise. Another wave of
coughing washed over her and she sat back down.
He grabbed her shoulder and heaved her to her
feet. She groaned but stuck her sword out in front
of her. He wasn't sure he would get much help in
the fight ahead but as long as she kept up, he could
manage.

He leapt past her down the last few steps. He
landed on the remains of the cot and the zombie
trapped beneath grabbed his ankle. He hacked its
wrist until it severed and hot blood spilled across his
foot. The house was packed with zombies, and
though they weren't charging, they weren't running
away, either.

Bayleigh had tried this and had similar results.
He'd known that. But Bayleigh hadn't had a sword.
He strode into the lounge and lunged straight for

the nearest zombie, severing a raised arm on the way to chopping its face in half. A cough signalled the arrival of Krystal as she appeared beside him. Her t-shirt still covered her mouth and her eyes were streaming with tears, but she attacked the next zombie with no less energy or effort.

They cut their way through to the front door until they had their backs to it. The heat was horrendous, sweat dripping from his eyebrows and stinging his eyes. The fire was coming through the ceiling, smoke flooding the lounge and pieces of blackening plaster raining down. The zombies weren't smart enough to dodge and some were knocked over by larger chunks of roof.

In a momentary lull, Luke snatched the front door open and fell through into the dark, clean air. Krystal was right behind him, gasping and dropping to her knees on the front path. He hauled her up, ignoring the burning in his shoulder. The zombies were closing, and the leader he'd seen from the window came running around the corner of the house, making a sound like a sea lion barking.

He thought about staying around to get rid of her, but they had only seconds before they were swamped. 'Run, RUN.' Krystal staggered in his wake and he hauled her past him and shoved her in the back. She stumbled but kept her feet and picked up her pace. Arms clutched at them as they fled the burning house but none were strong enough to hold them.

The pack fell behind as they raced from the estate and up to the remains of the petrol station. The flames were gone from up here but smoke still trickled into the night sky, lit a dirty orange by the street lamps. He felt a wave of nostalgia. If he squinted it looked just a little like hell.

They reached the bikes, sprawled like corpses on the tarmac. He hauled his up and put the stand down then did the same for hers. The keys were still in the ignition and he got his running while Krystal bent over hers, coughing like her throat was bleeding. There was a chance it was, but she'd recover.

'Come on, come on.'

She glared at him over the handlebars and turned the key. Nothing. She did it again but the bike was dead. He looked past her. The pack were closing, the woman zombie out in front waving her arms and screaming. They had seconds before she reached them.

Bayleigh

The main room was packed, every one of the ladies crammed in and perched on desks or chairs. A crowd was gathered around one who was wrapped in a blanket, face blotchy and red. Bayleigh stopped, heart sinking. She didn't want to ask what had happened. In the event, she didn't need to.

'This is your fault.'

She blinked, looking around for her accuser. One of the ladies stepped forward. She was crying as well, her pale blue eyes swimming and bright beneath the fluorescents. Her brown hair was tied up, showing the strong set of her jaw and a long, graceful neck. Bayleigh swallowed down the burst of jealousy and tried to remember her name. She thought it might be Jenna, but couldn't be sure.

'I'm sorry, what's my fault?'

'This.' The woman pointed one perfectly-manicured finger at her distraught friend. How was she supposed to play this? She blinked again. She couldn't believe she was thinking about it in those terms. So much had changed in the last week, so many terrible things had happened, and now she was trying to manage fifty people. She hadn't done that since before she started the shop and even then, it had never been fifty.

But she could do this. She thought she could even enjoy it. And she loved that it took her away from what was happening outside. In here, with the ladies, she could forget about the zombies. She walked straight across the room, smiled at the woman accusing her, and knelt beside the crying one.

'What's your name?'

'T-Tilda.'

'What happened, Tilda?'

'Dave. I thought... he's really cute and we're all going to die so I thought we could... you know...' She looked at her hands where they twisted in her lap. Bayleigh took them and squeezed gently.

'Yeah, don't worry, it's fine. I get it. We're not going to die, though.'

Tilda gave her a long look with her eyes wide open. 'We aren't?'

There was so much doubt in her voice it almost wasn't a question. 'No, we aren't. I have no intention of dying. We have an angel looking after us who very much intends for all of us to live. And besides, why would we die?'

'Well, the devices are going to run out soon, aren't they? And then the zombies will come in and eat us.'

Her voice shook. The women were nodding at her words and Bayleigh nodded with them. She straightened, looking around the room and taking a deep breath. 'We aren't going to die. We'll be out of the city long before the devices give out. Luke and Krystal are finding food today, a warehouse filled with food. We take it and get out into the country where there aren't any people. There may be one or two zombies at most and we'll kill them long before they get anywhere near us. We'll be safe and sound. We can grow food so we can eat properly and we'll be fine. I'm not promising the best life in the world, but we aren't going to die.'

Some of the ladies smiled back at her as she gave them her best reassuring look. It would have been difficult to lie, but she believed what she was saying and they could tell. Then Jenna came forward. 'That's great, but Dave isn't coming.'

She wanted a fight. She wanted to make everything better and didn't understand that fighting Bayleigh wouldn't do it. So Bayleigh turned away and knelt back beside Tilda.

'What did he do?'

'He... he attacked me. He took his trousers off and I thought we were going to... then he just grabbed me around the throat and started strangling me.'

'It isn't good enough. We can't trust him.' Jenna interjected.

Bayleigh waved a hand behind her to shut her up. Not that it was working.

'Don't wave at me. He nearly killed her.'

'I know. But shouting at me won't make it better and I don't think Tilda needs you shouting at all right now, okay?'

She could hear her voice rise and swallowed the anger. She needed to be an example. The ladies weren't hostile towards her, not yet, but if she started shouting it could change very easily.

'Tilda, when he was, you know, attacking you, did he say anything?'

She shook her head. 'Nothing. He didn't even...' She looked down again.

'Yes?'

'It sounds stupid.'

'Doesn't matter. What was it?'

'He didn't even look human, like his face was all screwed up but it wasn't human any more.'

'He's a demon!' Jenna's voice cut through the fragile atmosphere of the main room and Bayleigh winced. This wasn't going well. Into the silence came the sound of the door opening, and Alex walked in. The ladies around Bayleigh stiffened and she groaned. The appearance of any man right now wasn't a good thing. She flashed her eyes at Alex, warning him off, but he came right on in and joined the fun.

'I've got Dave in the other room. He isn't going anywhere, don't worry.'

'He's a demon.' Jenna made sure everyone heard in case they missed it the first time.

'Yeah, I heard that. I don't think he is, but I think he's possessed by one.'

'Possessed?' Bayleigh couldn't stop herself. This was a self-confessed cynic of anything not proven by statistics talking about possession. Alex strolled across and knelt beside Tilda.

'You okay?'

She gave him a grateful smile and Bayleigh relaxed just a little. Score one point for the men. He stood again and turned around to Jenna. The pale-eyed lady had her arms folded and stood in the kind of posture a customer would take when they came to complain. She'd had all of three in the time the shop was open and every one had needed to vent, without having any real complaint.

'Something's wrong with him, he—' Alex began.

'Of course something's wrong with him, he tried to kill Tilda.'

'Yes, I know that. But it's not in his nature.'

'Not in his nature? He killed Sian.'

There were gasps from the ladies and Bayleigh rubbed her head. That was it, then. There was no way this was ending well. She had to try though.

'You have no proof of that. I don't believe Dave would have done that.'

'He just strangled Tilda. What more proof do you need?'

In truth, she didn't need any. She knew as well as they did that Dave killed her. She tried to imagine him pushing his fingers through her eyes and it was disturbingly easy. She shook her head.

'Whatever he has or hasn't done—'

'You mean you know as well as I do he's a murderer—'

'We don't know that—'

She was shouted down by more people than just Jenna. Alex raised his hands and waited for the shouting to die down. It took a while and Bayleigh spent the time trying to figure out where it would end. She hadn't by the time Alex spoke.

'I understand your anger, really. But this isn't just a normal attack. There's something wrong with Dave. I want to say clinically wrong, but I don't think that applies here. There's something wrong with him and we need to help him.'

'You can help him, but it won't be here.' Jenna stepped closer to Alex and wagged her finger at him. 'We can't let him stay here if he's going to hurt people.'

'What do you mean?' Bayleigh said. She already had a good idea what she meant, but wanted Jenna to come out and say it. Maybe then she'd realise the reality of what she was suggesting.

'He needs to go.'

'Where?'

'Out.' She thrust her quivering finger toward the window and Bayleigh followed the line of it, shaking her head. 'That's ridiculous. He'll be killed before he's gone fifty feet.'

'If God thinks he's worthy, he'll save him.' Jenna said, jaw quivering. 'If he doesn't then we've only hastened something already coming.'

Bayleigh sneered. She didn't mean to but Jenna sounded far too much like Jackson for her liking. Jenna saw it and pointed at her, looking around for support. 'That's what she thinks of us. She doesn't care about our safety.' She turned to the room, puffing her chest out. 'I say we find Dave and escort him out of this hospital.'

Bayleigh wasn't sure what she was expecting but it wasn't the resounding cheer that filled the room. She met Alex's eyes and received a helpless shrug in response. Jenna headed for the door and a large number of the ladies went with her. Soon Bayleigh and Alex were left with Tilda and a couple who had stayed with her.

Tilda shook her head and mouthed 'I'm sorry'. Bayleigh gave her what she hoped was a reassuring smile. It wasn't her fault. It wasn't anyone's fault. Jenna wasn't to blame either. She was a customer with a chip on her shoulder and the circumstances to turn it into something far larger and with serious consequences.

Bayleigh dashed from the room in time to see Jenna shove her way into another room. Moments later the ladies led a hapless and very much confused Dave out and down the corridor. He was pushed past Bayleigh and gave her a questioning look. She wanted to say sorry but she couldn't take her eyes off his perfectly clean hands. Hands that were almost pink from scrubbing.

Why hadn't she thought before? She'd been so sure it was Jackson, she hadn't even considered getting Dave to stay out of the way, somewhere he couldn't hurt anyone. It was too late now.

They followed the mob down to reception. The doors were open and a zombie was half in and half out, dawdling idly. Dave was shoved forwards and Bayleigh half expected the ladies to start chanting for blood. Something quite different happened instead.

She didn't see it, not exactly, but one minute Dave went stumbling into the reception area, and the next he stiffened, then threw himself at the zombie.

The reception went deathly quiet, save the sound of Dave slamming his fists into the creature's face. Within moments it was a mess of blood and bone, Dave sounding like he was punching wet mud. The blows slowed until they stopped completely.

Dave looked back at them and Bayleigh gasped. It was like he was wearing a skin mask, a different face laid over his own. Then the mask slipped, fading away until it was just Dave, bemused and staring at his bloody fists.

'See, can't you see?' She aimed it at Jenna but it was loud enough for everyone to hear.

'He's possessed, drive him out.'

She didn't know which one said it. It didn't matter. Now it was a witch hunt. The ladies surged forward and for a moment Bayleigh expected Dave to flip out and attack them. But instead he allowed himself to be driven back until the doors slid open and he stumbled out into the evening sunshine. The ladies backed away and the doors closed.

Bayleigh urged him to come back in. They wouldn't do it again, they couldn't. Just come inside. They could find a room away from everyone else and keep him there until Luke returned and they worked out what was wrong. Just come back inside. Dave took one look at the doors before he turned and put his back to them. He glanced around the street. Bayleigh saw at least one zombie on its way towards him, but Dave didn't wait. Without a backwards glance, he put his head down and ran.

Dave

He was broken. Had he thought that before? Perhaps he had. Not that it mattered. The only important time was now; memories were for other people, people who cared and worried. All he had to worry about was right now. Had he been someone who worried, he thought perhaps he'd be very concerned. But he wasn't.

There was a space in which to run, and plenty of spaces beyond that, so he went. He flew between the zombies like they were standing still and headed west, towards the centre of town.

He was the wind.

He wasn't sure where the thought came from, but it seemed right. It seemed real, like a remnant of a life that had, perhaps, been better than this one.

His feet thudded against the concrete as his mind went in circles. They'd driven him from the hospital because there was something wrong with him. He'd known there was, even if he hadn't wanted to admit it. He'd killed that woman and tried to kill the other. He knew it because of the way Bayleigh looked at him just before he left. There had been no doubt on her face.

Even at the end, she shouted something to try and stop them. But she hadn't tried hard enough to make him believe he was innocent. Why couldn't he remember doing it? Trying to kill someone was quite a drastic thing to do, surely he'd remember it. But then, he was broken.

If he was broken, he could be fixed. Perhaps he should text Az and ask him about that. He hadn't texted Az in a while, not since Luke and Krystal headed off to find the food. That was almost a full day ago. He knew a day had gone because the sun was slanting into his eyes, cutting between the buildings as he ran. Soon it would be gone entirely.

He should find somewhere safe. There was nowhere safe, not in the traditional sense of the word, but somewhere he could barricade and sleep. He was tired. His feet caught on something and he stumbled. He caught himself before he fell and kept going. He'd been here before. Running.

He was the wind.

His feet brought him from the no-man's land of the city into the west end and he stopped below the huge yellow boards advertising the Lion King Musical. His chest heaved and the stitch in his side felt like one of the zombies had taken a bite out of him. He could hide in here. He could get into one of the boxes and barricade the doors, and no one would be able to creep up on him.

He dashed up the steps, shouldering aside an usher dressed in black, hands clawing at him as he went. The foyer was empty save the two zombies sat in the ticket booths. They were trapped, their hands bloody from where they'd been bashing at the glass. They growled as he entered, their eyes fixed on him, but he ignored them as he read the signs.

The classy gold fixings were out of place alongside the zombie ticket-sellers. He followed the arrows towards the boxes and was halfway down the darkened corridor when he stopped. A monkey, or rather, a zombie dressed as a monkey, stepped into the hallway.

It wore a huge head dress and carried a staff, clutched clumsily in one hand. The moment it saw him it lurched forwards, stage paint cracking off its face. There was something about the patches of rotting skin showing through the blacks and browns of the paint, that made Dave hesitate. It was like it was trying to hide its zombieness. He thought that maybe he knew about hiding things.

That was all it took for the monkey to reach him.

The staff fell as its hands reached for his throat. He staggered back and landed on his arse. The creature landed atop him and its teeth opened wide. Dave giggled. He was being attacked by a monkey in a theatre in London. Something slipped in his mind.

It was like walking on ice. There was always that moment when your balance goes and you try to stay upright, knowing it's pointless. Memories came sneaking in, flashes of women he'd known.

As their faces filled his mind, the zombie closed its teeth over his arm. He stared, eyes wide. He was being bitten. He screamed and yanked his hand back just before it closed its mouth. He could feel the warm saliva on his skin, and the thing's panting breath, and the mist came down.

When he came round, he held the monkey's head in his hands and sat astride the stiff body. The head stared at him with wide, dead eyes. He threw it down the corridor, groaning and burying his head in the chest beneath him. It smelled so gross his stomach heaved and threatened to spew his breakfast across the dark carpet.

Did he eat breakfast? He'd found it harder to eat since St Paul's. He certainly hadn't had any lunch, and his stomach growled as he sat up. He clambered off the monkey and weaved his way down the corridor. He'd find the box, barricade the door, and sleep. Then he'd worry about food.

He glanced through an open door and caught sight of the stage. The front half of a giraffe slewed back and forth across it and he found himself mesmerised. He half expected to see guts dripping from the back end but it was just paper and card and wood.

He shook his head and traveled on. He reached the boxes without meeting any more animals, hauled open the door to one, and screamed. The zombie leapt forwards and grabbed his face. Its nail went through his cheek and he smashed his fists against it, driving its arms down and away from his body. His control slipped, but somehow, he was aware this time.

The faces were still in his mind, sharp and vivid, as though the violence was taking him back into his past life. He stood with the faces and watched himself as he fought. Though in truth, it was no fight.

He drove the zombie back into the box and grabbed its arms. He skipped around a chair and yanked the arms down as hard as he could. They struck the back of the chair and snapped off, leaving him holding the stumps. Keeping hold of the hands, he stepped back around the chair and beat the zombie in the face with the wet ends.

Battered by the relentless assault, it staggered away until it reached the edge of the box. He threw the arms over the edge and grabbed the creature by the material of its shirt. He hefted the zombie over the barrier, then leant to watch it tumble down. It struck the edge of the stage and exploded.

Its skull split apart, brains spilling across the stage. Its legs flew into the front row and its body collapsed into the brains. The mist receded and he backed away from the edge, stomach once more complaining. The giraffe lurched towards the body.

As the zombie bent to the corpse, the head and long neck of the giraffe struck the stage and broke off. It was forgotten, discarded as the zombie began scooping brain matter into its mouth. Another zombie, this one with an entire herd of gazelle attached to its head, came stumbling from the wings and sunk its teeth into one of the arm stumps.

Dave slumped into one of the chairs. He was up just as quick as he grabbed the door and slammed it closed. There was a lock! With a huge grin he flicked it closed and slumped back into his seat. He'd seen faces, people he knew he'd once loved. He didn't know what it meant to love someone, not now, but he knew it was important. Theoretically.

He tried to picture their faces. They had been so bright, so vivid when he'd been fighting, but now they were almost gone, dull shapes in his mind. He sat up, trying to find them. He squeezed his eyes closed and searched but there was nothing there. He wanted to see them. He wanted something! It was a strange thing. A feeling he couldn't blame on hunger. He took the feeling down into sleep.

His eyes opened slowly, cracking the film of crust that covered them. How long had he slept? The theatre was no different. He blinked and stared about. Some of the boxes on the opposite walls were busy, zombies sat in chairs or leaning against the balconies. One was busy tucking into someone who presumably had once been its date or wife.

He blinked and looked away, blushing as his stomach growled. He needed to eat. He glanced up and jumped. His chair wobbled and toppled backwards, taking him into the darkness at the back of the box. A zombie wearing tights and a lion's head was hanging from the box above, hands flailing around wildly.

Dave put his hand on his chest to try and slow his thumping heart. He groaned, eyes not leaving the lion. Any second it would drop from the balcony and tear into him. He tried to slide off the chair while keeping watch, but his shoulder slipped and he tumbled off. He scrambled up, hands over his head. The lion was still there and still twitching.

He waited, holding his breath. Its hands no longer flailed, only twitching like the rest of it. It jerked and Dave jumped back, cowering again. Then it moved. He watched, eyes wide as the lion finally pounced.

The first thing he saw was that there was no lion below the waist. Instead he saw the bloody loops of entrails and tattered edges of skin. The second thing he realised was that it wasn't attacking. It struck the edge of his balcony face first and the crunch drowned out his retching as its face split apart. Then it tumbled away and off the balcony, down to the stage.

He didn't rush forward to check. He took a step to the nearest chair and collapsed, unable to take his gaze from the bright smear on the railing that shone in the dim lighting. He heard a creak from the balcony above and peered up at the darkness. It didn't matter what was up there, it didn't know he was here. He pulled his feet up to the edge of the chair and wrapped his arms around his knees.

His stomach growled again and he clapped his hands over it. Surely the creature above had heard that. But the creaking was still occurring and he had a horrible picture in his mind of a zombie chomping down on the lion's severed legs. He shuddered and went for the door.

He listened for a while, but heard nothing. He needed a weapon. He needed something with which to defend himself instead of just his hands. He stared at the blood and gunk covering his fingers and knuckles. He should wash them. Preferably before he ate anything.

He slipped down the passage until he found the signs for the toilet. A zombie stood at the sink, trousers around its ankles, staring in the mirror. How long had it been there? Dave almost stood beside it to wash his hands. If not for the trousers, it could have looked almost normal.

There was nothing here, no weapon to speak of... he felt the mist this time, like a tube train's lights coming towards the platform from the tunnel. The ground shook and the sound grew louder and a wind blew and then he was driving the zombie's face into the edge of the sink. He slammed and slammed and the nose and cheek bones went. He knew the moment the sink smashed through to its brain, but he didn't stop. It wasn't until he felt the hard edge of the basin against his hand that he released the body and stepped away.

The zombie slumped to the ground, skull mostly gone. The skull was, in fact, mostly on his hands. It took a moment or two to come back to himself before he set the taps to blasting and started to scrub. Once the water stopped running red he dried his hands, visited the loo, and crept back into the corridor.

He hadn't seen the faces that time. He'd been searching for them as he debrained the zombie, but they were gone. The thought of never seeing them again made him want to vomit, his mouth opening and closing like a fish on the dry wooden slats of the quay. He needed food. Everything would feel better after food.

By the time he reached reception he had resolved to return to the theatre. The box was safe and it was warm in here. He could bring things back and make a place for himself.

He visited the co-op first, finding one with only a couple of zombies in, and beating them both to death. Both times he searched for the faces and both times he was unsuccessful.

He struggled back to the theatre with bulging bags and climbed the stairs to the top boxes. He went in the one at the furthest end of the corridor and locked the door. Then he sat down and ate until his sides hurt whilst watching dislocated flocks of strange birds weave their way across the stage. The zombie actor to whom they were attached ruined the effect somewhat by kneeling beside the corpse and licking at the semi-dried blood.

Oddly, his tinned food didn't taste any worse. Although, it would be a struggle to make it taste much worse. He needed a stove, some way to heat the food. There was a camping shop just down from Trafalgar square on the way to St James's Park. He stood, stretched, and headed for the door.

He reached reception again and grabbed a bag of popcorn from the desk. He tore it open before he stepped out into the street. He was getting careless. He knew it because he opened the door when he should have seen the gang of zombies stood across the road.

He did spot them, though, when the door opened and one of them, a zombie wearing what looking like a London Underground uniform, pointed at him. He was almost more surprised by the pointing than the horde of zombies rushing towards him.

Jackson

Jackson stepped out and smelt the air. It smelt of opportunity. He would kill some zombies today, and do it with a smile on his face. The view from up here was breathtaking, the whole of London spread out below him. He raised his hands like he was lifting a glass ball and cupped London between them. He held the whole city between his fingers. If he had an army he could wipe out the zombies, drive them before him and sweep them into the river.

He glanced over his shoulder. He didn't have an army. He had forty something scared young girls who thought they wanted saving when what they really wanted was dick. If they just did what Harriet had, and admit to their true selves, they'd find everything they need. He was sure of that, just like he was sure God had sent them to the Shard so Jackson could see this.

He spread his arms wide. This was his city. This had been his city since he was a little boy, escaping Mam's gaze for long enough to punch someone or sneak off and steal from the old lady next door. Now he was in charge. He didn't need to sneak around or pretend anything.

He winced as the bruises and cuts on his back strained against the stretching. He grinned and stepped back through the glass doors. Harriet was asleep, face pressed into the pillow. Her shoulder was naked and showed the marks from last night. Turned out she didn't just like to do the hitting; She liked it rough all over. Suited him down to the ground.

He dressed, not bothering to be quiet, and left the room. The remains of the food was stuffed into the fridges and he had a dig until he found something to eat. Then he picked up the baseball bat he'd found in the security office and headed for the lift.

The journey down took a couple of minutes, long enough for him to reflect upon the previous day's events. From stuck up Christian bird to animal man-beater in a day. He hadn't asked her who else she'd done it with. It didn't matter, and he had the strongest feeling he was the first. She didn't hit with any precision, she just liked whaling on him. And she liked it when he threw her around a bit and dug his fingers in.

He liked it as well. Never thought much beyond getting his end away but now it felt like a whole world was open before him. Although, he hadn't slept much for wondering whether God approved.

He'd prayed but received no answer, so he knew he didn't mind. He trusted Jackson, and he trusted Harriet also. She wasn't his chosen, but she was a true believer. She was responsible for separating the ladies and driving them away from Luke.

So if God approved, he had no problems with it. It wasn't written about in the bible, but then, neither were zombies.

The lift doors opened and he stepped out into the reception area of the Shard. It was a huge expanse surrounded by glass. It was one-way glass, the sort you could see out of but remained invisible while you were behind. It made zombie killing especially fun.

He waited by the door, watching the stupid things lurch back and forth. As one staggered past, he hauled open the doors, set his feet and took a swing. The bat crushed the creature's nose and drove it deep into its brain. It dropped like a stone to the floor and Jackson stepped back, letting the doors hiss close. Perfect.

He watched the others swarm until a small crowd surrounded the corpse. Jackson opened the door again and got stuck in. The bat was the perfect weight, and he got so much power behind it, the first zombie didn't know what hit it. The back of its head came away, stuck to the bat, and it toppled to the ground.

He got the next one in the neck and it went straight through, so the head spilled on to the concrete. The body thumped down hard, blood spitting and streaming from the stump. He stepped back and let the crowd go to work, cleaning up the front of the Shard.

The morning went quickly, a pile of bones bearing ragged scraps of flesh building up in front of the building. The zombies never stopped coming and Jackson's arms didn't stop moving. The sun was high when he saw something different. A truck, like those used by the soldiers of God, pulled up on the pavement with a screech of tires. Three men bundled out and started firing.

At first, Jackson thought they were firing at him and he threw himself to the floor. But none of the windows smashed and he peeked from his prone position to watch the soldiers pour streams of bullets into the zombies. He almost felt sorry for the stupid things. They didn't know to run or defend themselves, and one by one their heads exploded and they dropped.

He needed more ammo. They accomplished in two minutes what had taken him most of the morning to achieve. They reached the doors and yanked them open. Coming face to face with him stopped them short. They raised their weapons and lowered them again as he shook his head.

'Welcome to the Shard. Nice shooting.'

The soldiers slung their guns and shook hands, introducing themselves. The first was called Tony, the second Brandon. The last gave him a weird look, like he recognised him. He may well do. Maybe he was one of the bastards who tried to take him out in St Paul's. He applied extra pressure with the hand shakes. The man's eyes narrowed but he responded with just as much pressure until they both let go. His name was Zack.

He waved them to the lift, talking as they went. 'Not many of the ladies ready for this yet. There're a few who are up for it, but most of em are frigid or near as you can get.'

'I'm sure we can charm them.' Zack threw him a bright grin and Jackson sniggered. 'Yeah, sure. We'll see. Only three of you?'

'The... our leader suggested we come in small groups so as not to alarm the ladies.' Tony said.

'Your leader?'

'Az.'

'You can call him a demon, I'm sure he won't be offended.'

Tony looked at the floor of the lift, rolling his shoulders.

'Well, I'm sure the ladies will be bowled over by your confidence.'

They spent the rest of the trip in silence. He didn't like having them here. This was God's work. This was why the ladies were here. Today the work of repopulating Earth would really begin. But it grated on him having them in his space. He needed to talk to Harriet, make it clear to her she wasn't the

only one. They needed variety in the next genera-
tion but he could screw a few of them, surely?

That wasn't God's work. He shook his head as the
lift doors opened. Harriet wasn't good for him. She
was deviant. The hitting and the way her face
changed when she was doing it. She found more
pleasure splitting his skin apart than cumming. That
wasn't right. But she was with him, so he could control her and keep her safe, even from herself if
needs be.

The lift door opened and they strolled down to
the reception area. Some of the ladies were there,
lounging on chairs or staring out the magnificent
windows. They perked up when the soldiers entered and a few strolled over. Jackson cleared his
throat, thinking to say something, before he realised
he didn't have to. The ladies gathered around the
soldiers, chatting and giggling. Was it the guns?

He had a gun. Maybe it was the uniforms as well.
He slouched against the wall, folding his arms over
his chest and scowling as the soldier who'd looked at
him funny - he'd already forgotten his name - was
led away by one of the ladies. He looked different
somehow, standing straighter and walking with his
head held high. And his eyes fixed firmly on the
lady's arse.

Jackson sniffed. Something wasn't... he blinked
and shook his head. The soldiers were here and the
work had begun. He was doing his job, the job God

had given him. With a smile he strolled to the window and stared down.

He was sitting in the lobby when Harriet came out. She flushed when she saw him and scooted across, greeting the ladies as she passed them, touching a hand or a shoulder. Jackson watched the sway of her hips and the press of her tits against her top and despite knowing exactly what lay beneath, his breathing sped up as he imagined tearing off her clothes.

She pulled a chair out from one of the smart white tables that dotted the area and sat facing him.

'No one is to know.'

'Funny, cos I was about to announce it.'

'No one. Do you understand me?'

He grabbed the finger she thrust in his face and pulled her half off the chair. She dragged it with her so she was sat with her legs almost touching his face. It meant he could slide his other hand between her legs and pinch the soft flesh on the inside of her thigh. She moaned, so soft it sounded like a sigh, and he squeezed harder.

'No one will know. But don't think for a second you can tell me what to do. Do you understand that?'

She nodded, lower lip caught between her teeth. He pushed his hand further until he reached her pussy and ground his palm against it. She jerked forward on the chair, breathing ragged against his ear.

'Control yourself. These women look up to you.'

She growled at him but she was smiling through hazy eyes. He sat back, rearranging his trousers. 'Some soldiers arrived today.'

'Soldiers?'

'Some of the soldiers of God. The right ones. They've come to begin the work.'

Her eyes narrowed. 'What work?'

'We need to rebuild the human race. Your ladies were kidnapped for that reason. We're doing it differently now. They have a choice. But we still need to do it.'

'Is that why you and I?'

'No. But you will bear my child and be grateful for being the one chosen to give birth to the next coming.'

'Coming?'

What had he just said? His child was to be... tears filled his eyes as he stared up at the ceiling. Of course. It made sense. He was God's chosen and she was strongest among his disciples. Where else would God's representative on Earth come from? But to be responsible for the next Coming?

He felt the weight on his shoulders but he also felt the excitement, a thrumming in his veins that made him shiver and sit up straight. 'That's right. Our son will be God's will on Earth, made flesh.'

Her mouth dropped open, right before she slapped him. He wasn't sure if it was foreplay, but the scowl convinced him it wasn't. 'That's blasphemy.'

'Why? Joseph and Mary were ordinary people. I'm chosen by God to save the Earth, it makes sense I should bring the child into being.'

'But...' She shook her head, mouth opening and closing. Jackson was about to reply when he saw one of the soldiers come back into the room. It was the one who'd looked at him funny, wiping the side of his mouth with a thumb and sauntering like someone who'd just got his end away.

Jackson rose, ignoring Harriet's protests, and made his way towards the soldier. The man ignored him, beckoning to another of the ladies. She went willingly and Jackson's mouth fell open. They needed variety, what was this about? He drew closer and was about to complain when he got a good look at the man. He was gorgeous.

The moment the thought went through his mind he knew he was cursed. But he couldn't take his eyes off him. He felt Harriet's presence at his side and put a hand out to keep her there.

'Who is he?'

He scowled at Harriet. 'Just one of the soldiers. Come to do his duty.'

'He can do my duty.'

He grabbed her wrist and squeezed, hard enough to feel the bones shift. She whimpered and he put his lips up close to her ear. The others were watching now, though whether they were looking at him or the soldier, he couldn't say. 'You're mine. No one else's. Do you understand?'

She tried to pull away and he set off down the corridor, dragging her with him.

'Let m—'

He squeezed harder and her words cut off as she gasped. He glanced back and was relieved to see every woman in the room staring at the soldier. More than one was half out of their chair but he turned away and led his new lady back down the corridor. He could have all of them, but not Harriet.

They reached her room and he shoved her through the door. She tripped and sprawled, landing face down on the bed with her legs on the floor. He pinned her down and started to haul her trousers off. She was begging for it and the soldier's face faded as he drove into her.

Krystal

She turned away from the bike and went for her sword.

'Get on mine, get on the back.'

Her hand fell from the hilt as Luke pulled up alongside her. The space on which she had to sit was tiny, but she swung her leg over and pressed up against him. She grabbed the metal bar behind her just as he charged away.

She was going to fall. She was going to tumble off and be eaten. She pushed with everything she had and regained her balance, then clamped an arm around his chest. They shot away from the zombies and down the ramp onto the A2. The weaving began, in and out the stationary traffic. The wind tore at her hair, throwing it this way and that, and she soon gave up trying to watch where they were going.

Being on the back of the bike was like being at sea, tossed around by waves beyond her control. Dad had taken her sailing once, ages ago, and the only strong memory she had of it was feeling like this, of being out of control and at someone else's mercy. Despite everything that had happened in the last week, she hadn't felt like this. Not until now.

She pressed her head into his back and held on. She managed it for about five seconds before her stomach churned and she had to lift her head. It felt faster and wilder when she had her eyes closed and now as she watched the cars going past, it felt horribly slow. She expected a zombie to attack at any moment, reaching out from a car or appearing from behind a truck.

But the river came into view without anyone trying to kill them, and her breathing and nausea eased a little. The lights were still on for the most part and London glimmered as Luke turned right and drove alongside the Thames. Krystal had always loved the water at night. The dirt vanished in the reflections of thousands of street lamps and she lost herself there now, peering down into the darkness.

'We need to find you a bike.'

'Now?'

'Why not?'

'I'm tired and hungry, we've just escaped a bunch of zombies, your shoulder's knackered—'

'Actually, it doesn't feel too bad. I think the ride will make it ache tomorrow morning, but I can move it now without too much pain.'

'Okay, that pain? That's the signal for you to curl up in bed and not move. That's how your body works.'

She could feel his grin even sat behind him, but he shook his head. 'It's a weak signal at best. Speaking of which, I got a text a few minutes ago, can you reach my phone?'

She slipped her hand into his jacket and pulled it out. She was taken back to her early days on the street, where a phone meant twenty quid and fifty if you knew the right person. And pinched the right phone. She'd stopped it pretty quick. The police would ignore you so long as you were ignorable. Stealing stuff made you very much... norable? Whatever it was, they didn't bother with the cells for people like her, just a night stick across the head and a feel up if they were that sort.

'You'll have to stop, I'm not letting go.'

The bike cruised to a standstill, with the railing on the left and a hotel towering above them on the right. The road was crammed with cars and more than one had their drivers still in place.

'Is this the best place to stop?' She asked.

'Just look at the text, would you?'

She sniffed and brought the phone around.

Where the hell are you? It's all gone to shit here. Bay x

'She put a kiss.'

'What?'

'Oh, Bayleigh. Apparently everything's screwed up back home, but she still put a kiss.'

'What do you mean, everything's screwed up?'

She read the message and watched as his shoulders rose. 'What does that mean?' He asked.

'Dunno. We should probably get back, though.'

'Mmm. We still need another bike.'

'Why? Aren't we gonna take a truck or something to get out the city anyway?'

'I want to take bikes as well. We'll need smaller transport once we're out in the country.'

She sighed and stuck her fingers up at the back of his head. He gunned the engine. 'Hang on.'

She grabbed the bar just in time as he set off. They weaved, moving even more slowly now. 'Can you hold your sword?' Luke said.

'What, now?'

'No, next week, of course now.'

'Ooh, easy, play nice. Why?'

'Because we need to go slow and I don't want to have to stop. You can fend them off.'

She took a deep breath, wrapped her left arm around his waist and drew her sword. Almost immediately a zombie appeared, lumbering down the pavement. Luke drew close and she fought back the urge to lean away. She did anyway, a little, and the bike wobbled.

'Stay still. Just move your arm.'

'Alright, alright.'

She swung and the bike wobbled again, but her sword bit deep into the zombie's chest, knocking it away from them. The back of the bike didn't stop wobbling.

'Luke, bloody stop it would you.'

'I'm trying, I'm trying.'

He sped up and the bike straightened. They spotted another zombie, this one alternating between the pavement and the road. He was, or would have been, a hipster, with silly hair and tight jeans above a pair of converse. She gripped the sword, liking this more.

'Try and hit it in the head this time.'

She growled and stuck her tongue out at him. She got her feet solid on the pegs and lifted slightly off the saddle as she put all her weight behind the swing. She caught the creature in the neck and the sword went straight through. His sticky-up hair was flattened as his head struck the concrete.

She looked behind to see the body still standing for a moment, blood spurting from the neck, before it crumpled to the floor.

'We got him, we got him.'

Luke chuckled then slammed on the brakes. She thumped against him. 'What the hell?'

'There.'

She followed his finger to a bike lying on its side across the road. He weaved between the cars and pulled up beside it. She hopped off the back and stood, bent at the waist and sucking air until the shakes subsided. A zombie was heading their way and, as Luke jumped off his bike and moved to the new one, he waved at her to deal with it.

She had a second to reflect on the fact that in the space of a week, she'd gone from being a scared little homeless girl with a pocket knife, to standing on the edge of the Thames, samurai sword in hand, and trusted by Lucifer to kill a zombie. It was, all things considered, a serious improvement.

She attacked, smiling at the feel of the hilt against her palm. Her first strike went too low and cut through the creature's jacket-clad left arm. The arm hit the floor spraying blood and she jumped back. It lurched on, somehow unaware of the wound, so she charged back in. She thrust point-first this time, stabbing the zombie through the bottom of the mouth and driving the blade up into its skull.

She grinned in satisfaction as she remembered to yank the blade out before the body fell. A throaty rumble from behind told her Luke had been successful. She turned and inspected it. It was a BMW and looked exciting, the silver bodywork gleaming under the street lamps.

'It's far more powerful than your last one. You're going to need to be very cautious at first. And you'll need that, too.'

They looked together at the zombie stumbling towards them with thick leather gloves and a motorcycle helmet on. It was like some weird coming of age thing, where she had to kill the beast to claim her prize. Or in this case, her helmet.

The sword struggled a little with the leather, but her first blow still shattered its knee. It collapsed and she lined up her next blow, getting it in the gap between the shoulders and head. Her aim was sweet and the head rolled free. Luke sucked air in through his teeth and shook his head.

'Big mistake.'

'Why, it's dead?'

'Yeah, but you have to get the head out of the helmet now.'

He popped his visor up and flashed her a grin, before returning to his own bike. She sighed and picked up the head. It was far heavier than she'd expected and she struggled to lift it the first time. She knelt instead and looked in the bottom. All she could see was blood and the trailing remains of the spine and arteries and whatever else she'd cut through.

She rolled the helmet the other way up and thumped it on the top. She lifted it like she was try-ing to get a cake from a tin, but the head stayed stuck. She lifted the visor and shuddered at what lay within. The man had worn a beard, but it had come out in patches and was caught inside the hel-met. Lifting the visor dislodged all the hair, and she held her breath as flakes of skin and reddish-brown beard floated around her.

She flapped her hand to clear it all out, then pushed down on the forehead of the zombie, while tipping the helmet up a bit. The thing didn't budge. She was going to have to cut it out and there was no way she was putting it on after.

Krystal stood and shook her head. 'No way. Not gonna happen. We'll get one from a shop, it'll be fine.'

Luke shook his head emphatically. 'Not a chance. That bike's very powerful. You aren't getting on it without a helmet.'

'Well aren't you the father figure now?'

He ignored her and drew his sword. 'Hurry up.'

She sniffed but turned back to the helmet. She didn't want to cut it out but she wasn't sure what else she could do. She tipped the helmet over and, standing as far away as possible, dug her sword in and scooped out its brain. That she didn't puke was testament either to her constitution, or the fact that the last few days had been utterly insane and this wasn't at the top of the crazy list.

It came out in great chunks, red and grey mingling with something black she was sure was the source of the foul stench. A zombie had spotted the blood and came bumbling over. She kicked the helmet off to one side and went with it while the creature fell to its knees to scrape the brain into its mouth. Luke took its head off before she could lose her no puking record and she turned back to the helmet.

She pushed on the face through the visor hole until the bones cracked. She kept shoving, and the face imploded inwards until it looked like a prop from a horror movie. The smell got worse and she tried to hold her breath. She stuck her hand inside the empty skull and pulled out fragments of broken bone until the face was dumped on the floor.

With the integrity of the skull knackered, it was easy to break out the rest of it and soon the helmet was empty. She raised it aloft with a triumphant smile and pulled it over her head. It was too large, wobbling on her neck. And it stank.

'We use this till we get back to hospital, then you're finding me another.' Krystal did her best to make it an order and he nodded slightly as he gestured to her bike. It was only once she was astride, the tips of her toes barely brushing the ground, that it occurred to her this could be very dangerous and stupid. She gunned the bike and grinned.

She let out the clutch and squeaked as the bike flew forward. She clung to the handle bars, keeping the throttle open as she headed straight for a car. She leant and scraped past it, her scabbard banging off the door. She bounced straight up the kerb and snatched at the handlebars as the railings drew horribly close.

She veered off just in time and straightened up, bombing down the pavement. She didn't dare look behind to see whether Luke was keeping up. Her only focus was on changing gear without stalling or killing herself. They reached the Imax in no time at all and she pulled onto the bridge.

She broke out laughing at what lay before them. It was like something out of an alien invasion movie. Hundreds of long-haired men and women, clad in leather and denim, sat in a huge circle. It was the metallers they'd avoided on the way out, which in itself wasn't too bad. They could avoid them just as easily. What was freakish was the person stood in the centre of the circle.

He was a zombie, his face coming apart and dribbling blood onto his t-shirt. His hands were held up before him as if to protect himself, but he didn't have the co-ordination to manage it. One of the zombies lurched up from its sitting position, staggered towards the one in the centre and swung at it. Its clawed hand caught him in the side of the head and knocked him down.

A chorus of growls went up. They sounded like growls from a drunk bear, dribbling and falling from their mouths. The puncher sat back down and the circle was silent. Eventually the zombie in the centre rose to his feet, hands held above his head. This time, she realised, they weren't there to protect it. They were raised in triumph. And the grunts from the others were shouts of approval.

She turned to Luke, raising her visor with a sigh of relief as the smell of the river battled the stench inside the helmet. 'They're playing a game.'

'I'm sorry?'

She nodded. 'They're playing a game. The one in the middle has to see how long he can take the beatings for. I've seen it before. Only when I watched it, you might get everyone else's change if you lasted long enough.'

They gave one another sickened glances and turned their bikes around. At the bottom of the bridge, where they had only just come on, another crowd of metallers stood, staring straight at them.

'They aren't playing a game.' Luke said.

'Nah, I don't think so.'

With a roar of growls and gibbers, the zombies charged.

Alex

He turned to Bayleigh and shook his head. He didn't know what else to do. The ladies were heading back up the steps into the ward, subdued now they'd sent a man out to his death. Bayleigh ignored him and stepped straight through the door as it hissed open. Alex went with her, acutely aware of the lack of weapon in his hand.

'Bay, come on, come inside.'

'Where's he gone?'

'No idea. But we can't follow him.'

'Can't or won't?'

He gritted his teeth and looked at the sky. 'Look, if he's running, he might survive. If we were just running, we might as well. But if we're trying to follow him, we're screwed.'

She didn't turn around, just stared down the street. The zombies were closing in and Alex took her arm. She shook it off, scowling at him. 'We should have done something.'

'Like what?'

She groaned and put her hands over her face. He tried to soften his voice. 'Look, Bay, he survived the first night and we know he can fight now. At least we know that. Trust me, I saw him down here with the zombies. He's... he's pretty terrifying. I don't think you need to worry about him. Really.'

Still no response. 'Bay, please, they're coming.'

Finally she shook her head and looked back at him. He gestured urgently to the zombies, now only metres away, and she nodded reluctantly. He took her arm and she shook her head, smiling. Then she was gone. He blinked and she was back through the door. By the time he dashed through after her, she was at the stairs.

The zombies came in after, at least one wearing boots that clicked across the floor. He took the stairs two at a time, puffing when he reached the top. Bayleigh was already halfway down the corridor to the ward. He glanced back. There were ten or so zombies staring at him, clutching at the air with their withered fingers, and he shuddered. She'd drawn them in here, staying out there that long. Not that she seemed bothered. When had she got so fast?

He raced off down the side corridor and in through the door of the ward, slamming it behind him. They wouldn't have seen where he went. How good was their sense of smell? He wasn't sure they went for anything except blood. It didn't matter, the devices would keep them safe. He charged into the private room and slumped on the bed.

Ed was sat in the next one along, staring at him with wide eyes, book face down beside him. 'What happened?'

Alex shook his head, getting his breath back whilst deciding how he was going to tell Ed. Bayleigh came sauntering into the silence and sat across from them.

'What happened to you?' Alex asked.

'I got fast.'

'Just a bit.'

'It's the spell. I can't do anything else.' She screwed up her face like she'd been expecting to turn lead into gold. 'But I'm fast, really fast, and it doesn't tire me out.'

Ed's mouth was wide open and he shook his head. 'Show me.'

Bayleigh raised an eyebrow and Alex held his breath. She moved and he tried to watch her. He saw her blur as she went near Ed but then he lost her. When the blurring stopped, she was back in her place with Ed's book in her hand.

'Oh my god, that's amazing.' Ed beamed. 'You're like a superhero.'

'I'm really not. If I was, Dave wouldn't be out there.'

'What do you mean?'

Bayleigh met Alex's gaze and gave him a beseeching look. He sighed and rubbed his head. 'We think Dave might have hurt one of the ladies—'

'He did the murder, didn't he?'

'I don't know. Yeah, I think maybe he did. But we don't have any proof.'

'So why's he outside?'

'The ladies drove him out.'

'The ladies? Why didn't you stop them?'

Alex tried to keep his voice calm. 'In case you hadn't noticed, there are rather more of them than us.'

'But you're in charge, aren't you?'

Alex tipped his head back, rubbing his neck as he stared at ceiling. 'I don't think anyone's in charge, except maybe that demon and the angel back in St Paul's. Everyone wants to think they're in charge, but they aren't.'

'Oh.' Ed's face dropped and Alex stared at him. He'd chatted to him once or two in the last few days, but not enough, probably. He seemed to be taking everything in his stride, but Alex didn't really have a clue.

'I don't think we need to worry.' He said. 'They were just panicking because someone got hurt. I understand it really.'

'Yeah, it makes sense.' Bayleigh said. 'They just needed to deal with it in a more reasonable way.'

'So where's Dave now?'

Bayleigh stomped to the window and peered out. 'He's out there.' Alex said. 'And he can run and fight.' The words sounded weak even to him. 'Bay, I think we need to text Luke.'

'And say what?'

'Just explain things are a bit messed up and find out what time he thinks he's going to be back.'

'Shouldn't they have been back by now?' Ed said.

Alex squirmed at both the question and the way Ed emphasised the 'they'. 'Yeah, they should. I'm sure they're fine—'

'You don't have to protect me you know. I'm perfectly aware of what's going on. Stop acting like I'm not gonna get it when you lie.'

'I wasn't lying. But look, Ed, you're what, twelve?'

He nodded, lips pressed tight together.

'No offence, but do you really get what's going on?' Alex asked.

'There are a bunch of zombies outside who want to eat us. There are a bunch of 'adults' - he put quotation marks around the word in a way that made Alex grin - 'who are arguing over who gets to have sex with who and when. Everyone's acting all noble, or mad, because everything's screwed and they're trying to pretend they aren't. Yeah, I get it.'

Bayleigh turned from the window with a grin on her face. 'Well said.' She pulled her phone out and started texting.

Alex gave Ed a weak grin. 'Sorry, I didn't get much when I was twelve except spaceships and planes.'

'Yeah, well, you didn't have a zombie apocalypse or abusive parents to deal with, did you?'

'Which is worse?'

'Parents, every time. They...' He choked off, staring past Alex at the door. 'They weren't what parents are supposed to be. At least the zombies are doing what they're supposed to.'

Alex smiled but it felt wrong. Bayleigh slid her phone back into her pocket and faced them. 'Only they aren't.'

'What?'

She beckoned them over to the window and they joined her staring out at the dark city. There were more buildings without lights now. For the first couple of nights you wouldn't have noticed the difference, but as the circuits broke and power stopped working, there were more and more blackouts. The City in particular had big areas of darkness.

Bayleigh pointed at the street. There were zombies down there, same as usual. But as he watched, he noticed a pattern. The same zombies were making the same short journeys, back and forth from pavement to pavement. He counted twenty one of them, all going round and round in circles. There were another two stood to one side, not moving at all, but clearly watching the others.

They were thinking. Those two weren't trying to be covert, but just by their inactivity they made it clear they were doing something deliberate. He shivered, sweat trickling down his back. Another zombie was stumbling up the road weaving side to side, oblivious to anything but the obvious difficulty it had in putting one foot in front of the other.

Alex saw it just before it happened. The twenty were a web and as the zombie wandered into it, the trap closed. They fell on the creature and tore him apart, all of them leaving their preassigned paths to take part. The two watchers wobbled away from their posts and into the centre of the group.

What happened next was the creepiest thing he'd seen yet. The carnage made his stomach churn, but it was no different to what they'd seen over and over again in the last seven days. But as the watchers made their way in, the others moved aside, inviting them in. The body of the victim, arms and legs already gone, lay on the floor and the watchers fell on it, tearing huge chunks out with their teeth.

Once they'd eaten a little, they stepped back and their followers set to. They were in packs. Alex had already seen that. But now they were thinking and planning and leading. And following.

Ed turned from the window, face pale. 'They planned that. The zombie didn't stand a chance.'

'Anyone who goes through that bit of street doesn't stand a chance.' As the words left his mouth he looked back at the street. That was the way Luke and Krystal would arrive back. Were the zombies practicing? He shook his head. There was no way the zombies had seen them leave this morning and put this in place. No way at all. They were just hungry.

'We have to be careful not to overestimate them. This is hunting behaviour, it doesn't mean they're smart.'

'But surely we should be prepared and stuff?' Ed replied.

'Yeah, of course. Just don't expect them to start acting rationally or in a logical fashion. They're still zombies.'

Ed climbed onto his bed and shook his head. 'Only they aren't, not real zombies. They think too much.'

Alex couldn't disagree, so he didn't. He leant back on the bed and looked at the cover of Ed's book. Stephen King. Kid had taste. Bayleigh flumped onto the bed beside him and snuggled into the crook of his arm. It was altogether too close and too sudden for him to be ready. He stiffened, his breath catching in his throat.

'You okay?' she asked.

'Yeah, just. Sorry, not expecting that.'

'Oh sorry, I'll just—'

'No it's fine, really, I—'

But she'd already moved, sliding over onto Ed's bed and sitting up against the pillows. He didn't want to look and see the hurt expression he was sure was there, so he examined his finger nails instead. Then he remembered what they'd seen at the window.

'Any reply from Luke?'

She checked the phone and shook her head. 'But if they're traveling back he won't be able to check it. I wouldn't worry.'

'I'm not, I just... the thing in the street outside. They'll be coming straight through that.'

Bayleigh went white and leapt up, racing to the window. 'They're still there.'

'And they will be when Luke and Krystal get here.'

She turned to him, putting her hands over her mouth. She pulled her phone back out of her pocket, pressed a few buttons and held it up to her ear. She began to pace up and down and he leant back against the pillows. After what felt like an age she took the phone away from her ear and stared at it.

She put it back again and kept pacing. She took it away, hammered at the screen for a few seconds, and then put it back again. Still no answer. With a loud out-breath, she shoved the phone in her pocket and shook her head.

Ed sat forward. 'What can we do?'

Alex slid off the side of the bed and joined Bayleigh at the window. 'I think if we kill those two, the others will leave, or at least, stop being so organised.'

'So how do we do that?'

Alex turned to Bayleigh. 'How fast can you go exactly?'

Dave

He stared at the finger being brandished at him. Zombies were, as far as his relatively limited knowledge went, without discrimination or specific interest beyond the search for brains. These zombies weren't limited to only brains, but beyond that, they seemed pretty standard. Now, though, there was one pointing at him and the five stomping his way were very clearly taking their orders from the dead dude in the tube uniform.

He leapt back into the foyer and slammed the door closed. Unfortunately, they were the type that opened both ways. He backed away towards the windows where the two ticket sellers still banged at the glass in their feeble attempts to escape.

He was exposed and open to attack from all sides. This was not a good situation in which to find oneself. He would stand more of a chance in the street. He could run in the street. He dashed back through the door, appearing right in front of the nearest zombie.

The mist came down and something surged within him. It felt like heartburn before he realised it was excitement. He reached for the zombie with both hands and found its claws. His hands closed over them and he squeezed. The fingers collapsed beneath his grasp and three snapped clean off.

The zombie reeled back, yanking its ruined hands away, but he went with it and caught its wrists. It growled, but it sounded more like a cat than a lion. Its struggles weren't enough to keep him from twisting the wrists hard and yanking them towards him. The skin split with a lurch and blood fountained towards Dave as he stood with the zombie's claws held in his hands.

The creature continued its pathetic mewling, but it charged anyway, flailing at him with its stumps. He beckoned it on, stepping between its arms so their faces were only inches apart. Its mouth opened and it lunged. He slammed his forehead into its chin. The impact rocked him but the chin shattered beneath his blow and the zombie staggered back.

Dave took a step back to survey the damage. He saw the blood streaming from the wrecked chin. He also saw the other zombies closing from all sides. He'd got himself trapped. Some part of him realised this, but his lust for violence didn't care, or didn't want to know. Either way, he ignored the approaching zombies and launched himself at the one he'd attacked.

He wrapped both hands around its neck and hauled it forwards. The zombie stumbled and fell, its stumps hitting the ground. Dave straightened his back, tightened his arms, and the weight of the falling zombie tore its head off. He lifted it and smiled at the now-blank eyes and the streams of lumpy blood dribbling from the neck.

He rolled it in his hands, grabbed the ears and spun around. The nearest zombie took its friend's head in the face. Dave swung again and again, slamming his new weapon into the zombie's nose and eyes. There were the predictable cracks and snapping sounds and Dave hit it harder. On the next swing, one of the ears tore off and he lost his hold. The head flew away and the zombie he'd been attacking came struggling on, face a mask of blood and hair.

Dave stepped around the swinging arms and shoved it hard in the back. The zombie dropped face first to the floor and Dave drove the heel of his boot into the thing's head. He remained with one foot planted in a mess of blood, brain and bone while he readied himself for the next attack.

But it came just a little too fast. There were two of them and they came from either side. He dodged one's hands, but the other grabbed his head and shoulder and its claws dug into the skin of his scalp. He ignored his attacker and went for the other one, grabbing the arms that had come past him and slamming them down onto his outstretched knee. They snapped off at the elbow and he kept hold of them.

The de-armed zombie staggered away and Dave turned his attention to the one trying to tear his head off. In the second he had left he jammed the bloody end of one of the stumps into its open mouth. The zombie's eyes rolled up like it'd just been given ice cream and its hands fell away. Dave stepped back, gasping for breath.

The part of him that was still screaming sat inside his head throughout the whole thing. He watched the fight unfold like a movie. Something was doing this, something that wasn't him. He couldn't fight like this. Faced with five zombies he'd run and run some more. But whatever was controlling his arms and legs was enjoying this, revelling in the destruction.

So was he.

He didn't want to admit it, and he didn't think he could feel anything. But the churning he'd named excitement had risen a notch. Now it filled him, a throbbing, overwhelming feeling that swamped his normal thoughts. All he could focus on was the zombie with stumps where its arms should be. It was coming back at him and he wanted it to come.

He slammed his foot into its belly. Something split and a smell, far worse that normal zombie smell, assailed his nose. He winced and drove the same foot into its knee cap. The joint shattered, the zombie took one more step, and collapsed to the floor. With a huge grin, Dave drove the heel of his boot into the creature's temple and felt a click of satisfaction as it struck the pavement beneath.

The zombie to whom he'd given the snack was crouched on the floor, gnawing its way through the arm. Dave nipped back inside the theatre and grabbed the fire extinguisher off the wall. As he came back out he saw another seven zombies closing in. They saw him and paused, hesitating as he reached the corpses.

Were they scared? He didn't believe that. But they'd just seen him kill three of them in fewer minutes. Were they cautious? The thought made him worry anew. Where were all these feelings coming from? He didn't worry, because he knew it was a waste of time. He merely allowed his future plans to be affected by the potential before him. But now he was worried, and perhaps he was right to be so.

They were displaying signs of awareness. Only basic, primal awareness, like animals who shy from the water hole when the alligators are there. But it was a step forwards in their evolution and within only a week or so of their birth. He wanted to shout at himself to run and get out of there, but it would make no difference. His body was in sway to something, or someone, else and he could shout all he wanted.

He hefted the extinguisher, holding it out for the approaching zombies to see. One was still brave enough to sneak in and steal the other arm. To its credit, it also snagged a hand on the way back. The original feasting zombie seemed oblivious to it all, still working its way through the arm.

Dave went behind it, sized up the shot, and took a swing. The head tore from the neck and went flying, hitting one of the waiting zombies on the way. It was enough to break the deadlock. The zombies surged forwards and Dave reached into himself. There was someone there. He could feel an alien presence, so he snarled and beat at it and suddenly, it was gone.

He almost fell as he retook control, his limbs suddenly heavy and sluggish. After his grace of moments ago, he groaned at his newfound clumsiness. But he could still run. Dave threw the extinguisher at the incoming zombies and raced away. A glance back revealed the zombies falling face first into their dinner.

Dave stumbled and picked up the pace. He'd almost stopped and he was still surrounded by zombies. This part of London was heaving with them, tourists carrying tattered maps in their hands, or pulling wheelie suitcases.

He ran through the bottom of Soho towards Piccadilly Circus and reached the street with the camping shop on. The doors were closed and the lights were off. He shoved on the door and swore. A sign hung in the windows, explaining that for no good reason they were closed on a Thursday. The plague happened on a Thursday. Was it Thursday today as well? It seemed like it might be, and wouldn't that be poetic in a horrible, sick sort of a way?

He had to keep moving. There were two bins at the edge of the pavement. He raced over to them and grabbed the first around the rim. He twisted and heaved and eventually unclipped it from its base. It felt heavy enough as he staggered back to the shop. The street was wide enough to give him a few moments before the zombies reached him.

With a roar as his shoulders screamed, he hurled the bin at the shop window. It bounced off and came right back, bumping into his foot. He looked down at it, swore, and set off running. Claws grabbed his shirt as he went.

He did a lap of the block, drawing them after him. When he returned to the bin he was alone for long enough to scoop it up again. Another throw and this time the window made ominous creaking and cracking sounds. He picked the bin up by the rim and kept hold while he swung the other end at the window.

The glass cracked like a spider web, but it stayed in place. He swung again, feeling the burn in his shoulders. It cracked further and on the next swing, the bin went through and lodged in the glass. He could have screamed. It would be a pointless thing to do, but the glass was ridiculously reinforced, as though someone had known he would do this and done everything they could to frustrate him. He ended up smashing it in chunk by chunk. By the time the hole was large enough to climb through, the zombies were closing.

His heart was hammering as he scrambled in. The glass cut the side of his hands and the growls from outside grew louder as they smelled it. He would have to get out of here at some point, but he could worry about that in a minute. As his foot touched the floor, the growls were obscured entirely by a howling siren that made his teeth ache.

He clapped his hands over his ears, which made very little difference, and staggered into the shop. He could see a keypad behind the desk with a flashing red light, but without the necessary code, he couldn't do anything about it. This floor was all clothing so he raced upstairs. He found a rucksack into which he put two stoves, some gas canisters, a knife, a small axe, a sleeping bag and, back downstairs again, some clothing.

He swung it onto his shoulders and bent double, taking deep breaths as the weight tried to shove him onto the floor. He couldn't run with this, not like before. He climbed back up the stairs, head ringing, and found the walking poles. He picked out two of the heaviest and sat for a moment. He was tired again already. His eyes flickered for a moment and he contemplated having a nap. But the window wouldn't hold.

Dave peered through the front window. The zombies were backed away to the other side of the street. They looked the same as when they were near the device, pushing against an unseen barrier.

The alarm. The sound, which he was nowhere near getting used to, must have driven them away. It was useful, up to a point. The idea of having to travel around with this sound made him want to vomit.

The top floor of the shop had a fire escape. He pushed open the door and headed out onto a narrow, black metal staircase that ran down into a tiny street behind the shop. All he had to do was make it back to the theatre. Then he could lock the door and sleep.

He took careful steps down to the street below, hefted his walking poles, and set out.

Bayleigh

She wanted to laugh at him. The idea of her going out there was ridiculous and made her stomach clench into knots. But maybe he was right. She'd spent the morning being grumpy about Krystal being chosen to scout with Luke. She'd spent the afternoon being excited about discovering this amazing ability, and through it all she'd been dealing, or trying to deal, with a murder and a bunch of angry church goers.

Maybe getting out and doing something proactive was just what she needed. 'What do you suggest?'

She could feel Ed's and Alex's eyes on her. Had they been expecting something else? The corners of her mouth drew up. She wasn't used to surprising people.

'I don't know. I just thought if you could get out there safely and we could figure out how to kill them...'

'We could just shoot them from here.' Ed said. 'If I had a sniper rifle...' He shifted across the bed, pretending to point a gun through the glass.

'That's not a bad idea.' Alex replied. 'Where are there guns?'

'No idea. The guards at the palace would have them. The police might have some, at the station.' She pulled her phone from her bag and went on maps, finding the nearest police station.

'Hold on. Before you go running off miles away, can we think about the original idea? You need something sharp enough to stick straight in their heads without slowing down.'

Ed's face brightened. 'We could make stakes, like in Buffy.'

Bayleigh laughed and nodded. 'Takes me back to my student days.'

'Isn't Buffy a kid's show?' Alex said.

She and Ed turned to glare at him at the same time. He backed away, hands raised in defence. 'Fine, sure, whatever. So stakes. We need wood and a knife.'

'Why not just a knife?' She asked. 'Any idea how much of their brain we actually have to skewer?'

Everyone shrugged, so she decided to go with that. She'd find out, one way or another. A few minutes later they were crouched outside the room, watching where their hallway met the main corridor. The zombies were in the hospital now, but hadn't found them, which was just fine. The longer they could keep their hiding place a secret, the better.

Bayleigh had four kitchen knives stuffed in her belt. Two of them were closer to normal dinner knives, but they were long enough to go most of the way through someone's brain and plenty sharp enough considering how easily the zombies broke. She took a moment, reflecting on the fact she was thinking about the relative merits of different knives for the task of stabbing someone to death.

She shook her head and turned to the others. 'Get back in the room and watch from the window, okay?'

'Not a chance. I'm coming down to the front. It's too far away up here, I'd never get to you in time.'

She smiled, cheeks reddening. 'That's really sweet, but you wouldn't get to me in time anyway. It would just be a waste.' She wanted to add that they couldn't leave Ed alone. Luke and Krystal should be on their way back, but if they weren't, she wasn't convinced about leaving Ed with the ladies. She wasn't convinced about leaving Alex with them either, but that was for very different reasons.

Alex gritted his teeth and explained that he was coming down whether she liked it or not. His cheeks were flushed and she realised she might have embarrassed him. Tough. Now wasn't the time to be over sensitive.

'I'm not waiting for you. I'm running the moment I leave the field, so I won't be able to protect you.' Once you've done the damage, why not twist the knife?

'I think I'll be just fine. Ready?'

His eyes wouldn't meet hers and she sighed. 'Ed. Head back to the room. If we die, keep trying to get in touch with Luke and Krystal, right?'

He nodded, lower lip wobbling.

'Hey, it's fine, I'm not gonna die. But just in case, you know?'

'Yeah.'

He walked away, not looking back until he reached the door to the private room. Then he glanced back and raised a hand before disappearing inside.

'Right. Let's go.'

Without waiting for him, Bayleigh rose to her feet. She was about to run when Alex grabbed her sleeve. 'Hey, hold on.'

'What?' Her stomach was doing flips. She needed to go, she needed to get this done. Alex obviously saw it on her face, because he swallowed whatever he'd been about to say.

'Nothing, just, be careful, alright.'

'Yeah, of course, you too.'

She dashed down the corridor and out to the landing. Zombies still cluttered the reception area by the front doors and she paused at the top. What had he been about to say? She knew exactly what it was so why the hell did she stop him? She shook her head and charged down the stairs.

She raced past the zombies and had to wait while the front doors hissed open, skipping from foot to foot. Then she dashed into the street. It was easier in the dark. The zombies weren't always obvious but neither was she. She paused in the shadows beside the hospital.

From here she could see the trap, the zombies lumbering back and forth on their assigned paths. They had even cleared the remains of their last victim from the centre so it wasn't obvious. The two leaders still stood near the wall, watching, waiting.

She flew across the road, aware of how fast she was going because of how quickly the opposite wall came at her. She put her hands out to stop and almost yelped as she thumped into the wall. The wind was knocked out of her and she flattened her back against the bricks, breathing hard. Sweat trickled down the side of her face. They were everywhere. The trap was where it were supposed to be, but there were other zombies as well, stumbling this way and that. Any moment they might smell her.

But she could run. She could run and never stop. She could run to safety. She could leave now and not come back, just leave the city and run until she found a mountain with not a soul around. And she could stay there.

She sucked in more air and pulled one of the knives from her belt. She could do all that. Or she could kill two of the bastards and prove to Luke she deserved the sword. She could prove to herself she was capable of more than just running a shop and looking after Dad.

What would he have thought about all this? She was glad he died before the zombies came. She tried to imagine him lying on his bed, Jungle Book on the TV while he chewed on her arm. It brought bile to her throat and she swallowed it down, then burst out coughing. She covered her mouth to drown out the sound, eyes flicking this way and that.

She tightened her grip on the knife and edged along the wall, drawing closer and closer to the leaders. She wanted to run straight past and not even stop, but she wasn't convinced it would work. She wouldn't know until she got there. She had to get there first.

She stared at her feet and legs, willing them to move. But the butterflies in her stomach had moved down and they felt like jelly, barely holding her up. With a sneer, she jabbed the knife into one and jumped on the spot. She tried to imagine it like a sporting event. This race was for the gold in the two hundred metres. She was Usain Bolt. She grinned. She was faster than him.

Her legs moved and she was running, the ground blurring beneath her. Before she had time to draw breath she reached the leaders and went past them. She thrust the knife and it was wrenched from her hand. She kept going, resisting the urge to punch her fist in the air. She'd done it, she'd actually done it.

She ran back into the darkness at the edge of the street and turned. Both leaders were still standing. One was looking, with a frown on its face, at the knife protruding from its belly. She blushed in the darkness and swore under her breath. She hadn't quite done it. But she would this time.

She knew she should hold off for a moment, give them time to forget they saw her, but if she waited, she might not go again. She dragged the next knife from her belt and ran. She slowed as she neared them, enough to get a bead on the nearest one's head. It saw her this time and she was going slow enough to deliberately plant the knife hilt-deep in its eye. She raced away and reached the shadows in time to turn and see the zombie collapse in a heap.

The horrible twisting in her gut transformed, and she giggled and gasped. She'd done it. She'd killed them before, but this time there'd been no struggle, no impending sense of being about to die. She was in control. She stared up at the windows of the hospital, trying to find the right one. But there were four with people in, all staring down at the street. Zombie watching had become a national pastime.

She guessed which one she thought was Ed and Alex and stared up at them. They confused her in equal measure. She blinked and looked away. Not now. The other leader hadn't moved, except to kneel and chew on his companion's hand. That made it even easier.

She sprinted across the space between them, wind whipping the strands of hair that had escaped her pony tail. She barely slowed this time and drove the third knife straight down into the top of its head. She kept running, heading away from the hospital down the street. She didn't want to stop.

She was buffeted as though she sat astride a motorcycle, the wind loud in her ears. She needed to find some way to measure her speed. Perhaps she could race Luke on his bike. That thought brought her down from her high and she slowed, nipping up an alleyway into the darkness. She stopped, heart racing.

Calm down. There was zombies everywhere. She could run fast but it meant nothing if she tripped over. They would eat her nice and slow and she couldn't run without feet. She shuddered and slipped down the alleyway, peering out the way she had come.

A zombie lurched through the darkness towards her. It was pulling something behind it that jerked and bobbled from side to side in time with its steps. Something flashed blue beneath the street lamp and she realised it was the tufty remains of dyed hair that clung tenaciously to its peeling scalp. The old

woman came fully into view, her granny bag trun-
dling along behind her.

Bayleigh tried to imagine what her face looked
like before the plague got her, but she couldn't see
it being much different. The zombie paused and
spotted her, grimacing to show a set of surprisingly
good teeth. It shuffled across the concrete towards
her and Bayleigh stepped back into the alley.

She couldn't kill an old lady, she just couldn't. But
it wasn't an old lady any more. It had been, but now
it was a zombie.

She stepped back further, leading her into the alleyway. The creature - she had to think of it as a
creature - came on, one hand leaving its bag to claw
for her. Bayleigh hauled the knife from her waist
band and set her feet.

There was something horribly comical and grotesque about it. It was like kicking one of those
small, pointless dogs people had. Or used to have.
But she couldn't miss the teeth that flashed in the
dim light. She glanced at her knife. Last one. She
wanted to keep this.

She jumped, trying to make it as sudden as possible to give the zombie no warning. She slammed
the knife straight into the side of the old woman's
head. There was a brief moment as she pulled it out
when the woman turned to her and she thought
she saw normal, human eyes that pleaded with her
and asked why she'd killed her.

Then she fell into the darkness, her skull cracking against the stone. Bayleigh swallowed the saliva that filled her mouth and knelt to wipe her knife on the old woman's clothing. Her bag had fallen as well and she found herself opening the lid. She flapped it shut, staggered away into the darkness and lost her lunch.

When the retching stopped, she slid the knife into her belt and headed away from the dead zombie and the bag. There were some things she could never un-see and never forget, no matter how hard she tried.

She dashed out into the street and headed for the hospital. She was so desperate to be away from the hell that existed out here on the streets, she almost ran straight into the trap. She spotted a zombie turning and staggering back the same way he'd come and with the lit hospital windows above, she realised where she was.

She did a u-turn, feet sliding across the tarmac as she changed direction. She knew how close she'd come because moments later a zombie wandered in from the opposite direction and was torn apart, metres from where she'd stopped. She picked up a couple of pursuers, more ambitious zombies trying to keep up. She raced away, doing a lap of the block before returning to the trap from the other side.

The leaders lay where she'd killed them, already being feasted on by others. But the majority of those in the trap were still there, moving back and forth on their paths. It was like they'd been programmed and would do this forever. Perhaps it was the promise of food. A primal instinct that told them if they kept doing what they were doing, they wouldn't go hungry.

She paused in the shadows, watching. So long as Luke and Krystal didn't turn up, it didn't matter. She pulled her phone out and checked the screen. Nothing. Where were they? She hesitated. Should she go back in the hospital? She didn't want to because she was useless in there. Out here she could do something. She just had to figure out what. At least she had time.

She got no further with her planning as the rumble of motorcycle engines grew rapidly louder.

Luke

They were being attacked by Metallica's fan club. As an observer of human life for hundreds of years, there were many things he'd been exposed to. But even before that, music had played a part in some of the horrors he'd inflicted in Hell. Taste, the human tendency to like and dislike, gave the average demon more ammunition than any amount of physical pain. Metallica he didn't mind too much, though his experience was limited to the occasional burst overheard from head phones.

Now he would be quite happy if the world had never heard of the band. He gunned his bike and checked on Krystal. She hadn't stopped amazing him the entire time they'd been out and she wasn't showing any signs of doing so now. He was stronger, faster, and fitter than anyone else on Earth, by some distance. She was a normal human, and a skinny, malnourished one at that. Yet here she was, still standing and smiling with it.

'Could we just ride at them, shouting?' She asked.

'I'm not sure that would work. Hang on.' He jumped off his bike and pulled off his leather jacket. The jumper underneath came off as well. He pulled the jacket back on then twisted the jumper into a roll of material. He unscrewed the petrol cap on the top of his bike and stuffed his jumper in until only a little poked out the top.

Krystal tapped her handlebars, one eye on him but the other watching the horde coming rapidly closer. He checked as well, nodding in satisfaction. There was still forty feet between them and though it felt like they were moving fast, they weren't. The pushing and shoving slowed them further.

'Can you ride with me as passenger?' He asked.

'What are you going to do if I say no?'

He shrugged. 'Push you off and steal your bike?'

She laughed and shifted forward on the saddle.

'Be ready. We're heading down the left side and there'll be flames, okay?'

She nodded and flipped her visor up. Her confident body language belied the tension in her face as she hid it from view. She was close to exhaustion and he couldn't blame her in the least.

He pulled his lighter out and held it to the end of his jumper. It smouldered a little but refused to catch completely. This was going to be tricky.

He shook the bike, making the petrol slosh around inside. He could feel it when he squeezed the jumper. That would have to do. He started the engine and slipped it into first gear, keeping the revs up as it started to move. He jogged alongside as he approached the zombies. Krystal appeared on the far side of the bike, cruising at the same speed.

'Get back a bit, just in case.'

She blanched but did as he said. He got his lighter out again, struggling to control the bike with one hand. It was only the forward momentum that kept it up. The zombies were much closer now and he could hear their growling over the revs. He gunned the throttle as far as he could, flicked the lighter and held it to the jumper. The second the flame flared into life, he revved once more and shoved the bike forward.

It wobbled but kept straight for a few yards. Then the balance went and it toppled over.

It didn't have time to hit the ground.

The petrol exploded as Luke threw himself back. The bike was transformed into shards and chunks of metal flying all directions and he threw his hands over his face. The zombies sounded like wounded animals, an eerie moaning sound rising from those nearest the explosion.

Amongst the debris hitting the floor he was pleased to spot a few, bloody limbs. Krystal pulled up alongside, grabbed his shoulder and heaved him to his feet. The world spun and it was all he could do for a moment to just cling to her and not fall over. It stabilised and he slung a leg carelessly over the bike.

'Ready?'

He mumbled something close to yes and they took off, powering across the tiny space between them and the horde. Krystal charged straight through the cloud of black smoke and flames. The bridge the other side of the explosion looked like a slaughter house, with pieces of zombie scattered among pools of blood.

'Pretty good work.'

He nodded and gripped the back bar tighter. The spinning had almost stopped but the smoke wasn't helping. There was a hole through the zombies and Krystal aimed for it. A couple of them reached out as they passed, but for the most part they were more interested in finding parts of their shattered comrades to chew on. Luke swallowed and his eyes dipped for a moment. His ears were ringing and the need to vomit became a coughing fit that made the bike shake.

'Stop it, I can't bloody hold it.'

He held his breath, trying desperately to suppress the coughing. They were past most of the zombies and safety lay seconds away. Then three huge figures appeared in the gap before them. They all had what was left of their hair down to their waists, and were covered in tattoos. The ink stood out against their pale skin and looked better than it probably ever had when they were alive.

They opened arms the size of small trees and Krystal hauled on the handlebars. He watched in silence, having no better advice to give, until he realised they were heading straight for the edge of the bridge.

'Stop, stop—'

It was far too late. He should have prepared for this, but his mind wasn't working quite as fast as he'd have liked. There was a chance he was tired as well. The bike struck the kerb and mounted the pavement sideways and airborne. They hit the top of the railing and flipped straight over it. He got one last look at the zombies on the bridge, staring in wonder at them as they hurtled through the air, then all he could see was the dark, soupy water coming up to meet them.

He managed to take a breath before they struck. It was cold. It was beyond cold, sinking straight through his clothes and numbing his limbs. He tried to kick to the surface but he was working at half speed. He couldn't open his eyes for fear of what foul sickness he'd get from the Thames, so he just kicked and kicked and hoped.

His lungs were bursting, refusing to hold the air in any longer, and the first bubbles burst from his mouth. He pushed them out and kept his lips closed, but the next lot he couldn't control and water flooded in. The moment it touched his tongue his control slipped away. He thrashed about, using everything he had left to drag at the water and pull himself closer to the surface. Except he didn't know where the surface was.

He opened his eyes and stared into the murk. He could see nothing. Then a hand reached up towards him and he grabbed at it. Krystal. She needed him. He tried to pull her up but she resisted, hauling on his hand. The water was filling his lungs and he was weakening every second. He was going to kill them both.

Krystal kept pulling and he went deeper into the water. Only there was light below and suddenly the world righted itself as he burst out into fresh air. The water shot from him in a fit of coughing. He went straight under again, but came up quickly and took another lungful. Something was grabbing him and he struggled.

'Stop, bloody hell, take it easy. Just let me help.'

He tried to relax, but his body felt as stiff as a board as Krystal's arm came around his neck and her body appeared beneath him. He let her pull him through the water towards one of the huge concrete islands that held up the leg of the bridge. They reached it and she took one of his hands, putting it onto the concrete.

'Can you hold on?'

He didn't know how to answer that, so he tried and found he could. 'Yes, I'm alright, I've got it.'

She let him go and swum beside him. They clung together to the island and he looked at her through blurry eyes. 'You saved my life.'

'Not the first time, I might add.'

'How?'

'Always been good at swimming. Not done it much in the last three years. Lucky I remember how.'

'But you did more than swim.'

'Yeah, well, mum always wanted me to be a life-saver. Thought it was important. Dunno why.'

'Maybe she knew.'

'Knew what? That one day I'd have to save the Devil from drowning in the Thames?' She chuckled and shook her head. 'I doubt that very much.' She paused. He wanted to say more but all his breath had gone. He rested his head against the concrete. It was quiet here, safe and peaceful. He could just have a sleep and—'

'Stop it. Wake up, you lazy sod. You gotta find me a new bike.'

His eyes flickered open and he nodded. 'Yes, a new bike.' It seemed incredibly funny and he laughed. Then he coughed and water came up that went out his nose. He coughed some more and vomited a little, but by then he was fully awake.

'Can you swim, at all?'

'I think so. I've never tried it.'

'You've never tried it. How old are you?'

'I'm not sure. I lost count after the first couple of thousand years.'

'And you've never tried swimming. Bloody typical. Give it a go, swim over to that island.'

He stared across the dark water to where she pointed. He could see the water rushing beneath the bridge as the tide headed out to sea. There was no way he was going to make it, none whatsoever.

'I can't do that.'

'The devil can't swim a few measly metres. I'm disappointed.'

'I'm still alive and intend to stay that way. Sorry.'

She sighed and nodded. 'Fine, I'll see what I can do. Always wanted to drive a boat.'

Without another word she set off, swimming hard against the current. There was only one island between them and the edge of the river and Krystal covered it in no time. She climbed out and he watched the water stream from her in the light from the South Bank. She looked a little like one of the smaller beings in the Dome.

He'd never bothered find out who or what they were. Something to do with one of the smaller religions, paganism maybe. Faeries or sprites or some such. A dying breed and not much use to anyone. He thought, in that moment, that Krystal was the most beautiful thing he'd ever seen as she emerged from the Thames in a shower of water that lit up white. When he got back to the Dome, he would spend some time getting to know them.

When he got back to the Dome... he'd been so desperate for that, for all the time he'd been here. But he hadn't been here that long and already he wasn't sure if that was what he still wanted. He'd never felt like this in the Dome. This feeling of being on the edge, of not knowing whether he'd see the sun tomorrow. That feeling was as strange as the pride he felt watching Krystal. Stupid, meaningless pride that somehow meant more than his chamber and his list.

From his vantage point, he could see the zombies wandering this way and that along the tow path. There was nowhere safe for Krystal to climb out. She scooted along the tiny beach below the hoardings and slowly vanished from sight into the darkness.

She wouldn't leave him. She was going somewhere to get a boat and come back. His feet were numb. He knew they were there but he couldn't have moved them if he wanted to. He needed to get out of the water. He gazed across the space to the bank and shook his head again. It was suicide. He looked up. The island was solid concrete, sitting maybe four feet out of the water. He should be able to haul himself up.

He stretched and grabbed a tiny ledge that jutted out halfway, then kicked with his legs and pulled at the same time. His feet felt like they had weights tied to them and his hand slipped off the ledge. His head went under and he came up gasping. He grabbed for the concrete again and clung on, as the cold sunk into his limbs and the water swirled carelessly past.

Jackson

He zipped up and stormed out of the room, leaving Harriet tangled in her trousers and glaring at him with ill-disguised lust. He slammed the door shut behind him. She needed to take the hint and stay put. She wasn't coming out while that soldier was here. Who was he? Jackson was going to find out and it didn't matter if he was dick-deep in one of the ladies or not. There was something wrong about him.

He strode into reception and stopped. The ladies were gathered together near the corridor. They were waiting for the soldier. They may as well have been queuing up with signs on their chests saying *slut.* He growled and stomped towards them. They saw him coming and didn't react at all. That was wrong. They should mind him.

'What are you doing?'

'We're waiting.' The nearest said, still not looking at him.

'I noticed that. Who for?'

'Him.'

Her eyes glazed over and Jackson took a deep breath, shoving his hands deep in his pockets. He didn't hit women, not anymore. Not unless they wanted it.

'You can't.'

She finally turned away from the corridor and stared at him. Her eyes looked drugged, the pupils dilated and hazy. She shook her head. 'We can't what?'

'You can't screw him.'

'But that's what he wants.'

'I'm sure he does, but you can't. We have to have diversity. If you all have children from him, what do you think will happen when your children have children?'

They stared at him blankly and he snorted through his nose. 'You need to all have children from different men or your grandchildren will be mutants. This isn't about who you want in your panties, it's about saving the human race.'

His voice rose and by the time he finished they were paying a little more attention. He grabbed the first lady by the arm and led her away to a couch. 'You can wait until the next lot come along.'

He went back to the row and got the next one. She was coming with him until a sigh erupted from the row. He spun around to see the soldier coming out of the room, satisfied smile on his face. He hadn't bothered replacing his shirt this time and Jackson saw the red hair raging across his chest.

'Az?'

The soldier smiled, more broadly this time, and Jackson caught sight of fangs that ended in sharp points. The women sighed again and Jackson threw himself at the demon. He grabbed him by the lapels and drove him against the wall. Despite being slammed into the plaster, the soldier burst out laughing.

'Why are you wasting your time? They want me.'

'They can't have you. What are you doing?'

'Me? Hasn't Luke told you? No, I don't suppose he has. Well, I'll leave it to him to say. Let go of me.'

The tone of his voice changed, from casual conversation to an order. Jackson almost let go. Almost. Instead he yanked him away from the wall and slammed him back. The demon's head bashed into the plaster and his teeth snapped together. Az growled and freed himself from the dent in the wall.

Jackson stared wide eyed as the demon lifted him off the floor and set him down a few feet away. Then Az punched him in the stomach. He folded over the punch and went hurtling back. He bounced off the opposite wall and slammed onto the floor. A couple of the ladies rushed over to help him to his feet. At least some of them recognised his authority.

He panted, trying to find breath. His back was on fire and one of his legs had twisted as he fell. He limped towards Az, but the demon was no longer paying him any attention. He was staring at the next lady in the queue, sharing a smile. How could she not see the predator before her?

Jackson limped close enough to talk without the ladies hearing. 'Get out.'

Az turned, one eyebrow rising, to look at Jackson. 'You got up. That's impressive. I'll hit you harder this time.'

'You can hit me as many times as you like, God will protect me.'

Az snorted then seemed to notice the woman who'd swayed over. 'He might at that, just to piss me off.' He stepped closer, lowering his voice for Jackson alone. 'The old bastard doesn't care about you. You're delusional, Jackson. The only thing you've been chosen for is to make our mutual friend's life just a little bit harder. If I wasn't enjoying the game so much, I'd kill you now and end it, but I haven't been this entertained since the old wanker shut Hell.'

He raised the other eyebrow, challenging Jackson, and he wasn't going to back down. With a roar he slammed his fist into Az's face and the demon was thrown onto his arse. He looked up at Jackson with wide eyes. 'Not ba—'

Jackson's foot followed his fist as he kicked Az full in the face. His dodgy leg gave out and he stumbled against the wall. But the demon was on his back, blood streaming from his nose. Jackson dropped to his knees beside him, shoved apart the hands coming up to block, and drove his fists into Az's face again and again. He felt teeth give way and cut into his fingers, but he kept going, kept piling on the hurt.

The ladies were shouting at him and one even grabbed his shoulder. He was vaguely aware of shoving her away, but every part of him was focused on ending the evil thing lying before him. He would beat him until his brains were spilled across the floor and his ladies were safe. Every time he raised his fist, he saw a mask of blood and nothing more.

Something stopped his fist.

One of the demon's hands caught his, and squeezed. The pain took a moment to sink in; his hands were already numb. But when it did, he screamed. His little finger gave way, snapping and crushed into the skin of his hand. His ring finger went next, the knuckle tearing out the top of his hand. The sight of his bone, white against the blood that coated his fists and the red of the demon's hand, made him retch.

Then the ladies started screaming. The sound was high-pitched and piercing and horrible and he had a split second in which he managed to yank his hand free of the demon's grasp. As he stepped back, Az rose to his feet.

They weren't feet anymore. Cloven hooves ended legs that reached to Jackson's chest and held up the true demon.

The ladies ran screaming down the corridors and Jackson was left alone in seconds, facing Az. The demon's face was screwed up along with his fists. 'You really piss me off. I want you to know that.'

Jackson didn't see the blow, not even when it cracked the bone that ran around the side of his eye. He flew across reception, flipped straight over a table, and landed on his neck on the other side. He peered beneath the table at the beast stomping towards him and gritted his teeth. He hauled himself up the table until he was standing, swaying.

He blinked and his eye exploded in pain. He was going to die here, beaten to death. The ladies would be defenceless and Az would take them one by one.

This was the end of the world. Not the plague, nothing that had come before. This was it. And it was down to him. This was why God had chosen him. It wasn't his smarts or his skills. It was because he would refuse to quit and refuse to lie down.

He grabbed the table and lifted it off the floor. The legs folded up and, as the demon reached for it, Jackson smashed it into his face. Az stepped back and Jackson got a better hold on the table, wielding it with both hands. He slammed it edge first into Az's nose and the demon growled, shaking his head like an impatient lion.

'Stop wasting your time.'

'The ladies won't take you now, not now they know what you are.'

'Do you think that matters? Do you think I care whether they're willing? It's more fun that way, admittedly, but I can live with either.'

Jackson roared and slammed the table into Az. This time the demon batted it aside and it flew from his hands. Az backhanded him across the face and he smashed into one of the shoulder-level partitions that divided up reception. He flipped straight over and landed on his back on another table.

That blow had been lighter. Either the demon was tired or growing weaker. His face appeared over the partition, smiling at Jackson. His hands followed it and grabbed him by the front of his shirt. He hefted him into the air and slammed him on his side across the partition. He felt a rib crack and gasped as the air was smashed from his lungs.

Az lifted him again and tossed him across the room. He slapped into the floor and slid through a pile of chairs, covering his face as they toppled down onto him.

'I can play with you for a while, you know. There's no reason to end the fun quite yet.'

Az crossed the distance between them frighteningly fast. Jackson was barely on his feet before Az grabbed the front of his shirt and dragged him in close. His breath smelled of iron. Jackson coughed.

'If I kill you, Luke loses all hope. If I keep you alive, he could spend years trying to get back.' He scowled. 'I don't intend to wait years.' Az looked up at the ceiling, his anger becoming thoughtfulness. 'But what's the rush? We've waited three hundred years and I can do this anytime. Why not enjoy it a little while longer?'

Az slammed his fist into Jackson's gut and though it was far gentler than the last blow, his rib jolted and he screamed again. Az chuckled. 'The zombies make it so interesting, too. Seph's gonna be pissed I didn't finish with the ladies, though.'

His musings were brought to an abrupt end by a strident voice booming across reception.

'OUT, DEMON. I CHARGE YOU TO LEAVE THIS PLACE, IN THE NAME OF OUR FATHER AND LORD.'

Jackson wanted to laugh. Or cry, he wasn't sure which. He peered sideways, realising he'd lost the sight in the damaged eye, and saw Harriet approaching, cross held out before her. The other ladies came behind her, chanting in time, and the sound filled the high-ceilinged room.

Az let go of Jackson and he slid to the floor, seeing the world sideways. Then the demon burst out laughing and spread his arms and wings wide. His presence filled the room, dominating everything, and the ladies stuttered and fell silent.

'Who's next? Who wants to fuck me next? You were all queuing up not long ago.'

'Begone, demon. You are evil and I demand that you begone in the name of God.'

'Yeah, in case you hadn't noticed, he's not listening all that much right now. Who're you? I didn't see you before.'

Jackson saw the leer on his face and growled deep in his throat. With a roar he surged to his feet and grabbed a hold of one of the demon's wings. He was half lifted from his feet, but his weight dragged it down and he felt something give.

Az tried to spin, but Jackson clung on, yanking it this way and that. He could feel it tearing, like working a leg free from a roast chicken.

'Get off me, you little shit.'

Jackson grinned through the blood running down his face. When had he started to bleed? Az stumbled away towards the windows, shaking his entire body as he went. Still Jackson clung on, his knuckles white against the vivid red of the demon. The pressure of his broken fingers against the hard bone of the wing frame made his vision blur and his stomach heave.

Az reached the window and drove his fist through the glass. The immediate rush of wind made a sound like an aircraft taking off. The demon grabbed the strengthened glass and tore it out, heaving the massive sheet into space. The wind that came rushing in stole Jackon's breath and left him gasping.

Az flapped his wings, dragging Jackson off his feet and towards the window. As he swung, the demon reached around his body and grabbed Jackson by the leg. He hauled on him but Jackson refused to release his wing. With a snarl, Az drove vicious claws deep into the flesh on Jackson's thigh. He screamed, his last vestiges of air fleeing his lungs.

The world spun and his grip on the wings weakened. The demon lashed them about and Jackson tumbled off. Growling in triumph, Az lifted from the floor and beat his massive wings. Jackson grabbed again but succeeded only in brushing the wing tip. He staggered forwards but lost his grip. His gaze left the demon and looked straight forward, at the yawning window right before him.

Az flew through it and out into the night sky. Jackson stumbled, tumbled forwards, and felt the wind take him. He twisted his body desperately, turning away from the window, but it was too late. He fell out into space, the lights of London twinkling far, far below.

Krystal

The sound of waves took her back. When she first got to London she spent a lot of time by the river, watching the world go past. There was something about the weight of history carried by the dark water that made the aching in her gut and the screaming in her head quieter. It didn't fade entirely, but tide and time eased the pain.

She'd never been keen on history in school. She hadn't studied much before she left, but she already knew she didn't like it. Coming to London, living in the shadow of buildings that had stood longer than anyone could remember, had given her a new appreciation of things. She'd sneaked onto one of the river cruises and sat near enough a family that anyone checking would think she was with them. They went up and down the river and she'd learned all about how important it was to London. She'd learned about Fleet Street and the Tower and days when the streets were full of shit and disease.

Being homeless in those days must have been so much worse. After, she'd spent weeks on Embankment just staring into the water and imagining her life a hundred years ago, or two hundred years ago. Now as she paced through the darkness, lapping waves on her left and the growl of zombies to her right, she was reminded of those times and shook her head. Had those really been the bad times?

She knew where she was going. She needed a way across the river and she had to be quick. There were always a few motorboats tied up beside the floating restaurants, but she had to get across first. The tide was out and as long as she kept close to the wooden hoardings, she was safe from the mud. And the zombies.

She reached the next bridge soon enough and looked up. The railway bridge coming out of Embankment station was a huge thing made of rusty iron girders. It reminded her of the old black and white photos she'd seen of the skyscrapers being built in New York. It was high up and looked in no way safe. But there were no zombies there.

The hoardings had become a concrete wall, but it was ridged and covered in huge screw heads. She started up it, one hand hold at a time, ignoring the burning in her shoulders and the shivering that wracked her body. The growls of the zombies drew nearer and louder as she climbed, but they were still the other side of the wall. So long as she didn't go down there, she was fine.

She kept repeating that as the skin on her fingers was rubbed away and they started to bleed. Her foot slipped more than once and every time it did, her chest thumped against the concrete. Her boobs were killing by the time she reached the top and she got one leg over. She lay flat, straddling the concrete face down and sucking in oxygen.

The iron bridge was close above her and the light almost non-existent. She turned her head and peered at the path. She saw joggers, still wearing sweat bands and still running, a week after they died. There were families pushing prams. Some contained tiny zombie babies that made her stomach lurch and her face heat up. Others were empty and she wasn't sure if they were better or worse.

When her heart slowed and the burning in her fingers dampened to a low sting, she sat up and examined the bridge. The girders were far enough apart for her to scramble straight through. She stood, head going through the gap, and pulled herself up as quickly as possible. She paused, feet resting on the girder opposite, and listened. The growling hadn't changed.

It didn't matter, the zombies would never get up here. But she was alone. She was out in the city on her own and the thought of them getting her scent and coming after her was enough for her to almost wet herself. Her sword was still in her scabbard, despite the swim, and she gripped the hilt, drawing strength from it.

Krystal shivered. She needed to keep moving or her wet clothes would drag her down until she curled up on the girders and went to sleep. She pinched herself and set off. The girders were huge and plentiful and she made good time, glancing down into the rushing water every time she was stupid enough to forget not to.

She tried to see if Luke was still clinging to the island, but beneath the bridge was only shadows. He had to be. He couldn't die, that would be ridiculous. He was the Devil. The Devil didn't die. Except she wasn't sure if he was anymore. She only sort of understood what was going on, but she was pretty certain he was who he said he was.

Except he was human as well. And not evil. At least, not so she'd seen. She knew he messed with Jackson and Dave pretty badly, but they weren't exactly nice people anyway. He wasn't all fire and horns and stuff. The way he looked at her was nice, too. He cared, in a way that wasn't dependent upon her being any particular thing. She hadn't known what that felt like until the last few days, but now she got it from him and Bayleigh as well.

The north bank was approaching quickly and she focused on getting there in one piece. There were more zombies here and getting down from the bridge was going to be tougher. There was no handy wall beneath her. There was, however, the foot bridge that crossed the river right beside the railway bridge. There were zombies on it, but not many, and if she was quick she could run from them.

She clambered to the outside of the railway bridge and hesitated. Huge concrete posts thrust out of the river between the two bridges, ending at the same height as them in a flat platform. But there was a gap between the two, where single steel bars ran from the bridges to the concrete. It was only river beneath, but with the tide out it was a fall of twenty feet and she didn't fancy that, not twice in one night.

She climbed out of the girders and balanced on the steel pole. At least the top was flat. She swallowed and wiped the sweat that cooled as soon as it appeared on her forehead. Arms outstretched and staring forward, she scurried towards the foot bridge. The wind whipped at her as it rushed up the river and she swayed, but kept moving. The river was no longer a benign friend, but a greedy presence, eager to swallow her up. She tried to take slow, calming breaths, but couldn't stop panting. One step and then another, one by one.

She reached the concrete and collapsed, legs shaking and heart pounding like some rich businessman had offered her a seat in his car if she'd only... she sniffed, groaned and rubbed her face. There were some things she'd never miss.

She was halfway there and still not spotted by any zombies. The metal pole that connected the concrete to the footbridge was round and considerably narrower. This was the tough one. She contemplated what she'd do if she fell in the river. The most likely thing was that the tide would drag her away and she'd go under. She was too tired, this time around. It would be peaceful as the cold seeped into her and the world faded. It was be much easier than what lay ahead.

She grinned and shook her head. This was easy. This was all easy. She put her foot on the pole and stepped off the concrete. Immediately the wind seemed to pick up, snatching at her short hair and whipping it around. It ran greedy fingers through her clothes and teased and pulled. She kept moving, one step after another, but her knees were wobbling and she kept blinking as her hair caught her eyes. Every time she blinked, her balance slipped and she wobbled more.

Krystal knew she was going to fall just before it happened. She tried to bring her right foot around but she didn't move it far enough out and it caught the back of her left foot. For a brief moment she balanced, right leg flailing, then she went. She saw the water rushing up, then her chest struck the pole, her arms and legs wrapped around it, and she clung on.

She spun until her body hung beneath the pole. For a second she thought she was going to lose her grip, but her hands tightened around the metal and she clamped tight to it. She locked one foot over the other and hung for a moment, chest heaving and wondering whether she'd have any nipples left by the end of the night. Every part of her complained, but the more sensitive places screamed the loudest.

She went hand over hand, shoulders trembling as she snail's paced it closer to the foot bridge. One foot slipped and she almost lost it, squeaking as she tried to wrap herself back around the pole. She hauled her errant leg back up and resumed her anguished progress. She lost herself to the night, eyes fixed on the clouds above.

She found herself puzzling about the weather. It had been lovely this past week, but the clouds above signalled rain for tomorrow. She hadn't thought about it too much, which was unusual for her. Her entire life was dominated by the weather. They were supposed to be leaving for the country tomorrow. Would rain make that any harder? Of course it would, rain made everything harder.

Her hand bumped something and she almost let go to grab her sword. Then she looked up and realised she'd reached the footbridge. With a sob, she grabbed the far chunkier frame of the bridge and hauled herself up until she sat on the outside, legs dangling over the river that was somehow her friend again.

When the shaking subsided, she rose to a crouch and peered onto the bridge between the metal rungs. She could make out two zombies. One strolled in a suit up the centre of the bridge. It was more of a shuffle than a stroll, but the lean of his body made it quite clear what he'd been doing before he died. The other zombie stood behind a metal trolley still bearing plastic cups filled with roast chestnuts and almonds.

Did nuts go bad? She was tempted to grab some before she imagined the look on Luke's face. She opted for the other direction instead, towards the shore. She shimmied over the railing, and her feet touching the solid concrete was one of the nicest feelings she'd ever had. She ran, no longer caring if she was spotted. She reached the long staircase and saw two more zombies climbing them.

She jumped onto the silver railings and slid, leaning back to speed her descent. She pulled her sword out as she flew down and set her arm back in preparation for the blow. She hit the flat section halfway down and nearly went straight over the edge. Krystal flung out her hands and steadied herself, still hurtling down the railings.

Halfway down the next section she was near enough to take a swipe. The blade bit into the zombie's face and knocked it over. She didn't look back to see whether she'd killed it. Her eyes widened as the bottom drew rapidly closer. Her arms were held up to keep her balanced but now she grabbed hold of the rail to slow her descent.

The movement unbalanced her and she tipped off the rail, slamming onto her feet on the last few steps. She ran wildly and somehow succeeded in not pitching straight over onto her face. She came to a stop, heaving in breaths, and burst out giggling. That was awesome.

A zombie lurched towards her wearing Lycra and a cycling helmet, and she lost it, breaking out into another spate of giggles. It attacked, clawing at her with hands that could no longer grip the handlebars, and she lashed out, chopping both off and then stepping to the side. Her second blow sent its head, helmet and all, rolling across the pavement to bump into the steps.

With a nod of satisfaction, she raced down to the river and peered over the black wrought-iron railings. Two boats bobbed in the shadow of one of the floating restaurants. She punched the air, scrambled straight over the barrier, and ran along the wooden wharf beside the larger ship. She jumped into one of the boats and stared at the engine. She hadn't a clue how these things worked, but she'd seen people doing it.

There was a pull rope and beside it a lever she could turn. She turned it and hauled on the rope. She got nothing the first couple of times and was about to turn the lever back when the third pull got a coughing sound from the engine. She kept trying, yanking the rope as hard as she could and swearing louder each time it didn't work.

The engine caught, sounding incredibly similar to her motorbike. She frowned down at the water. Her motorbike that was now at the bottom of the Thames. She could find another, but she'd liked that one. She hurried with the knot that tied her to the quay, her shivering fingers feeling like sausages as she fumbled. Finally the knot slipped free and she took the handle protruding from the engine.

She squeezed what she hoped was the throttle. The boat darted forwards and thumped into the side of the one next to it. She grinned sheepishly and peered up at the bank. A couple of zombies were playing the audience, trying and failing to clamber over the railings to get to her. She turned away, got the boat pointed in the right direction, and headed out onto the river.

At first the tide dragged her away from the bridge. She put a little more power on and it pulled in the direction she wanted. She turned into the river and headed straight towards the bridge, only turning to the left as she drew near. The closer she got, the faster her heart went as she squinted for Luke.

He was there! Only his head and arms were above the water and he made no sign he'd heard her when she shouted. She drew the boat nearer and nearer until she could almost touch him. She didn't dare let go of the tiller. It felt like she'd go flying downstream the moment she let the power off.

'You're gonna have to swim and get in.'

His head turned slowly and she saw in the dim light his pale face and lips the same colour. He wasn't swimming anywhere.

'Can you just grab the boat? That's all you've got to do, just grab the boat.'

She got closer still and one of his hands came away from the island. He fumbled with the edge of the boat, fingers failing to close over it. Eventually he got a grip. There was a brief moment when Krystal struggled to hold the boat steady against the tide, while Luke was torn between his two places of safety. Then he let go of the island and grabbed the boat.

Krystal leapt to the front and the boat spun away from the bridge, turning a full circle as the river caught hold. The next bridge was coming fast. She knelt in the front and grabbed Luke's arms, trying to heave him from the water. At first he did nothing, staring up at her blankly. She glanced behind and saw the huge concrete posts looming large. If they hit one, the boat would fall apart and they'd be back where they started.

'You have to help, bloody help me.'

He blinked and the next time she heaved, he kicked and came far enough out of the water to get his chest over the edge of the boat. She pulled again and he slid agonisingly slowly over the side, his hands gripping one of the seats. That would have to do. She looked back again and screamed. The concrete leg was feet away and even as she threw herself towards the tiller, she knew she was too late.

Alex

They watched Bayleigh kill the zombies and disappear into the darkness. Ed groaned as she vanished, probably not even realising he was doing it. She'd returned soon enough, accompanied by a sob from the boy. Alex saw the pale skin that showed through his long hair and the hands that gripped the window sill like he was never letting go. They shouldn't be watching this. It wasn't good for either of them. Either she could do it or she couldn't.

She raced up the street and Alex realised she hadn't seen that the trap was still there. Ed grabbed his arm. 'She's gonna go in the trap.'

'Hang on, take it easy.'

He yanked his phone from his pocket, but it was far too late. Then she stopped, as if she'd somehow heard their frantic distress. She turned in that weird, elastic way she now had, and they both let out a long breath. Ed turned away from the window, shaking his head.

'She's going to die.'

'No she's not.'

'Yes she is. We all are. Don't lie to me, I'm not stupid. All we're doing is wasting time. Why not die now and get it over with? She should have listened to me.'

'Who? What did you say to Bayleigh?'

'Not her, Krystal. She should have let me finish it back at the house.'

'I don't know what you mean.'

'You weren't there, that's why, of course you don't know. But I knew it then. We're all going to die. Why are we prolonging it, like we've got a chance?'

He sniffed and scrubbed his face with his hands. Alex opened his mouth and closed it again. He couldn't find anything that might make this any better. There were no words that wouldn't sound like dissembling and Ed was right. He wasn't stupid, not at all.

Ed glared up at him, took another look out the window, and stomped from the room. Alex sighed, leaning his forehead against the glass. This was difficult enough without Ed freaking out. Probably better he wasn't here, though. He could find a room to hide in until Bayleigh came back. If he was lucky maybe he'd find some of the ladies to make him feel better.

Alex grinned. There were plenty of ladies here who could make him feel better. He looked out of the window and watched Bayleigh dash across the road. She moved ridiculously fast. It was like watching a movie on fast forward, only she was still graceful and smooth. Did she do *everything* fast now?

She hunkered down in the shadows and when he flicked his eyes away from her, he couldn't find her again. Why wasn't she coming inside? The trap. She had to stay there until Luke and Krystal came back. She had to warn them. It was a typical Bayleigh thing to do, thinking of others first.

Her entire life seemed to have based around that. She'd talked a bit about her dad in the last couple of days and it didn't sound good. Looking after him for however many years must have been tough. It sounded like he died only a couple of weeks ago, though he wasn't sure about the details. It had something to do with Luke, he knew that much.

He sighed and turned away from the window. He should go back to reception. He hadn't been able to see anything from down there and the zombies were too numerous to hang around so he'd come back upstairs. Now he wanted to go down and out into the street. Bayleigh made it look so easy, running back and forth and attacking people with knives.

He wouldn't find it so easy. Who would it help if he went down there and got himself killed? Was he a coward? There was a sixteen year old girl out there somewhere, armed with only a sword. Bay was down in the street with a butter knife to keep her safe. He was stood up here within the safety of the devices and still he was scared.

He sneered at himself and left the room. He could do this. He had to do this. He had to prove he was as worthy as the rest of them. Not as worthy, more worthy. After all, this was his fault. As long as they didn't know that it was alright. But if they found out, if Bayleigh found out, and he was hiding and staying away from danger, she'd have every right to hate him.

He reached the top of the stairs, baseball bat in hand, and paused. Three zombies roamed around reception, but it wasn't them that gave him pause. It was Ed, halfway down the stairs with nothing to defend himself. His head hung like he was already dead, hands swinging limp at his sides.

Alex wanted to shout but the noise would draw the zombies. He took the stairs two at a time and grabbed Ed's shoulder. The boy turned and Alex had to work hard to stand his ground. It was like staring at one of the zombies below. There was pain in the boy's eyes, and something else besides. He was pleading, begging for something, but Alex didn't know what.

'What can I do?' Why had he asked that? Ed shook his head and turned back to the zombies, trying to resume his descent. Alex grabbed him again but Ed shook him off.

'Get off me.'

'You aren't going down there.'

'Why not?'

'Because you'll die.'

'And?'

'And I don't want you to die. And neither does Bayleigh, or Krystal.'

'You didn't mention Luke.'

'You already know Luke doesn't and—' He cut off as the zombies heard his voice and turned. They lurched across the floor towards them. 'You know why Luke wants you alive. I'm not sure you get why Bayleigh and Krystal do.'

'Because they care about me. Because they want to protect me from the world and keep me safe and all that other bullshit.'

'Why is that bad? Why is that bullshit?'

Ed spun back around to face him. Tears ran from his screwed-up eyes. 'Because they can't protect me from me.'

Alex frowned. How was he supposed to handle this? What did the kid mean? 'What do you mean? What are you going to do?'

'My brain hates me. My brain thinks I should just go and kill myself. It's easy now cos I can just walk down these stairs and they'll do it for me.'

'You aren't going down those stairs.'

'WHY NOT? WHY THE HELL NOT?'

Alex ducked as his screams bounced around the huge space. Ed's voice cracked halfway through. Alex wanted to hug him, though he had no idea if that was the right thing to do. What was wrong with him? He smiled inwardly as he answered his own question. Ed was a teenager who'd come from an abusive home life and spent the last six months on the street. He was now living, or doing something resembling it, in the middle of a zombie apocalypse. That would do it.

Ed was stomping down the stairs again and he watched him go. He couldn't stop him, not without physically restraining him. But he could get rid of the zombies. Without them, Ed would have no choice but to live. Alex raised the baseball bat and stared at it. The end shook and he tried to convince himself it was just the weight.

He raced down the stairs, shoving past Ed without looking at him. He wanted to check whether he'd stopped, but he couldn't think about anything except the zombie lurching towards him. He raised the bat and tried to pretend he was Luke or Bayleigh. It came close enough for him to catch a whiff of the rot. That was far enough.

He swung the bat as hard as he could and struck the zombie full on the side of the head. The bat kept moving. In fact, all of him did, as the head tore free from the body and flew across the room. His swing completely over balanced him and he spun around to face Ed, bat bouncing off the stair rail.

The boy *had* stopped and was staring at him with wide, angry eyes. Alex didn't want to see them. He didn't want to see him at all. He wanted to be back upstairs, watching through the window to make sure Bayleigh was alright. But he hefted the bat and turned to face the next zombie.

He tried the same swing but this time caught it on the shoulder. The bat sank deep into its flesh and the sound of cracking bone was loud in the reception area. The zombie stumbled and fell, tripping over itself. Alex pounced, slamming the end of the bat into its face again and again. When the sound became that of the bat hitting the floor, he looked up.

The third zombie was already there. It grabbed him, claws digging into his shoulders. He twisted and squirmed until the hands fell away. He grabbed the bat in both hands and rammed the creature beneath the chin. It staggered away and he steadied himself.

He brought it straight over his head from behind and struck the zombie plumb in the middle of its skull. Brain erupted from around the bat, while blood squirted from its eyes and mouth and nose. Alex stepped back, covering his mouth as the corpse crumpled to the floor.

Reception was empty, save for him and Ed. Alex tried to flick the worst of the blood off the bat but it wasn't working. Screw it. He rested it on his shoulder, trying to ignore the smell and focus on what he'd just done. He could fight. He could be useful. He could make amends for what he'd done.

'What did you do?'

He jumped and turned to Ed. 'What?'

'What did you do. They were for me.'

'You aren't killing yourself.'

'I wasn't going to, they were going to do it for me.'

'There's no difference. You might as well have drunk poison by coming down here. The end result is the same. And Ed,' He stood at the bottom of the steps and stared up at him. 'You aren't killing yourself.'

'That's not your choice, that's my choice.'

'That's true. But this is about more than just you and me. You're the youngest person on Earth. You will live longer, probably, than everyone else. There'll come a time when you're the only person alive who remembers what happened here. You can't kill yourself.'

Ed's face dropped and he stared at his shoes. It looked like it was working. He wanted to say more, but he thought he might scare the kid. Better to leave it at that and let him reach his own conclusions.

'I'm the youngest person on Earth.'

'Yeah, weird, isn't it?'

Ed shook his head and whistled through his teeth. 'You can't be sure.'

'Of course not. But we're the only people alive except all the soldiers of God around the world and their hostages. So it seems pretty likely. Now can we go back upstairs?'

Ed stared at him and again he saw the pleading look. What did he want?

'Can I do anything?'

Ed shook his head. His hair came down to mask his face, the vulnerability hidden away once more. But he turned and trudged back up. Alex let out the breath he was holding and followed him. He was most of the way up when he heard the rumble of motorbikes.

Luke

The boat twisted and turned and he knew he should care. But he couldn't feel his legs and his arms were shaking uncontrollably. His teeth rattled together as Krystal dumped him in the bottom of the boat. She screamed and threw herself away from him, then the boat twisted and shot sideways, throwing her back on top of him.

The dark underneath of the railway bridge flashed by above before they were spat out beneath the streetlights of the South Bank.

'Oh God, could have done without that. Jesus. Right.'

He listened to her, waiting for something approaching sense to emerge, but she kept saying 'Jesus' and 'okay' and 'right' a lot, so he tuned her out and focused on his pain. There wasn't much right now, which he thought should be a good thing, but had a sneaking suspicion wasn't.

'I think I need to get dry.'

'D'you think? Next you'll be saying you want to be warm as well.'

She flashed him a grin he tried and failed to replicate. His lips felt like silly putty, all chunky and lazy. He pressed his fingers against his cheek and got only the slightest response. 'I think it needs to be soon.'

She hissed at him and put more power on, drawing the boat away from the centre of the river and back towards the north bank. She slowed it, keeping quiet as they nudged up next to one of the floating restaurants. She got the rope curled up at the back and threw the end to him.

'Tie us to the restaurant.'

He looked at her, waiting for instructions as to how he was going to do that with sausages for fingers. She ignored him, her forehead creased as she concentrated on keeping the boat beside the restaurant. It was like wearing really thick gloves. Not that he'd ever worn gloves.

He fumbled about but eventually succeeded in getting their rope behind the one that ran in loops down the side of the restaurant ship. He pulled it tight by grabbing it in both hands and falling to the bottom of the boat. They rocked but were dragged tight to the restaurant, the front of their boat lifted from the water. He wrapped the end of the rope around the post at the front of the boat and looked around.

Krystal was already beside him and balancing on the edge of the boat. She tucked one foot into the

loop of rope, shoved herself up, grabbed the side of
the restaurant and slipped over the rail out of sight.
Luke stared up, blinking. Was she coming back for
him? Why did he feel so pathetic? His brain was refusing to do anything more challenging than make
basic observations.

Krystal's face appeared above him and he beamed
at her. She gave him a look and shook her head.

'Get up and do what I did.'

He almost complained before something told him
that would be an unwise thing to do. He leant
against the boat and lifted one heavy leg into the
loop of rope. He heaved and went precisely nowhere. He tried again and felt something in his leg.
Unfortunately, it was a grinding, stabbing pain that
made him whimper. And he still didn't move.

The pain didn't stop and suddenly he longed for
the numbness. Krystal leant over the rail and offered him her hands. He grabbed them, pushed up
with his legs, and somehow she was pressing his
hands onto the rail of the restaurant. He clung to it
for a while, taking deep breaths, before he pulled
himself up.

He rolled over the rail and landed with a thump
on the narrow slice of deck. Krystal stood over him,
hands on her hips. 'Any chance you gonna man up
any time soon?'

He glared at her, wondering if she'd ever known
the kind of pain that was cutting through his legs.
She probably had. Still. He sat up and pulled his

knees closer, resting his head atop them. She gave him about two seconds.

'Get up. We need to get going.'

'I need to get dry.'

'You sound like Ed. Come on.'

She grabbed his hand and yanked him to his feet. He hobbled after her, every step sending bursts of agony through his legs. She found an open door and led him into the restaurant. Tables were crammed together and laid beautifully with knives and forks and glasses. And a zombie.

He wore chef's whites and staggered towards them, bumping off tables. Krystal went to meet him and Luke beamed again. She was ready now, for whatever came. She was a couple of tables away when she stopped. He could almost hear her thinking. Then she reached for a wine glass and threw it at the zombie. It broke over him and he shook his head about like a wounded bear.

Next she selected a knife, gripped it by the blade, and tossed it at the zombie. She missed. He heard her swear and go for another. This one hit him in the face, handle first and he shook it off again. Luke was about to remind her they were in a hurry when she scurried around the table so there was only one between them. She grabbed the edge of it and rammed it hard towards the zombie.

It slammed into his gut and he doubled over, chef's hat tumbling to the floor. Her sword appeared in her hand and she drove it straight through the top of his head. The chef stiffened and collapsed face first onto the table, then slid to the floor. Without saying a word, Krystal headed for the kitchen on the far side of the boat.

Luke was happy to find a chair and sit as his legs went from pure agony to sharp, intermittent stabbing pains. A moment later, Krystal emerged carrying a pair of white trousers and a chef's top. Luke stared at her as she weaved her way towards him through the tables. She'd gone, in a night, from being a scared sixteen year old to a capable young woman.

There was, he supposed, nothing like zombies to bring out the best in someone.

'Get your clothes off.'

Or not. He struggled out of his soaking clothes and stood shivering.

'Get dressed then.'

He pulled on the chef's trousers and top and felt a little better. 'What about you?'

'They're mostly dry already. Can't be arsed, there's nothing in there my size.'

She was already stomping to the door.

'Hang on a minute, can I have a minute, please.'

She turned, eyebrow raised, then came back and sat down. Her shoulders slumped as she put one elbow on the table and he realised why she hadn't wanted to stop. He wasn't sure he could get up, but she'd done so much more than him in the last few hours. He heaved himself from his chair, groaning as he put weight on his legs, and patted her shoulder. 'You saved my life. Thank you.'

She looked up at him through bleary eyes. 'Whatever. You ready?'

He chuckled and shook his head. Seeing her expression, he nodded. 'Yes, absolutely, sorry. I was just reflecting on how different you are to when I gave you the rose.'

'Well, I'm not homeless anymore.'

'That is very true. And you have a sword.'

She patted it and rose smiling from her seat.

Embankment was quieter than usual, only the odd zombie shambling along.

'Where've they gone?' She asked.

'The packs will be finding places to hunt. They'll come here when other grounds are empty.'

'They aren't on the bloody African savannah.'

'But the logic is the same. They will make packs and hunt down the weaker ones. After that...' He spread his hands palms up, and shrugged. 'What happens then? Will they grow in intelligence? In twenty years we could be fighting pitched battles. At the moment the weight of numbers is only a problem if you let them surround you. But give them weapons and it's another story altogether.'

'Well aren't you a bundle of bloody joy. Can we settle for getting back to the hospital tonight?'

They found another bike without much bother, got it started, climbed on, and went searching for a second. A few minutes later they found it. It was a police bike, huge and unwieldy, but with plenty of power. It sounded beautiful when he started it up. He caught Krystal grinning at him. 'What?'

'You're looking different, that's all. More human.'

He nodded, ignoring the frisson of doubt that ran through him. He didn't want to feel more human. He didn't want to lose the edge that meant he could do what he needed to. And he didn't want to become weak.

He was no nearer deciding what he would do with Az and Seph, but he would need his strength and he would need to be ruthless, regardless of which path he chose. He would be fighting either the Father, or two very powerful beings. Either way, the sticky human emotions that were gaining more and more control everyday were bad news.

But the bike sounded great. He revved the engine and they set off north, away from the river. He glanced down a side street and saw a pack. It was hard to tell in the gloom, but it looked like twenty or thirty zombies gathered around something on the floor. They were listening, silent in the dark of the alleyway, and his skin crawled.

They bypassed St Paul's. They needed to go back there soon. They would need to recharge their remaining devices and he wanted to know what the soldiers of God were doing. Without their own devices, they were trapped in the cathedral, tied to the machine. But how long would that last? He had the feeling Az or Seph had ordered them to leave Luke's group and the ladies alone, in an effort to keep him sweet, but they would be growing impatient.

There was so much he didn't know. The future was empty of anything except running and zombies and doubt. He hated it, and the very fact that he could find hate within himself frightened him. Nothing was worth hating. Hate got in the way and confused things, but he couldn't drive the panic from his mind when he thought about what lay ahead.

So he would go back to St Paul's before they left. But first he would go to the hospital and sleep. Krystal too. Her bike weaved a little more than it needed to and he imagined she was almost dead on her feet. They reached the road that ran past the hospital and as the building came into view, lights streaming from the windows, they accelerated.

Perhaps if they hadn't, they would have had time to slow or even stop, when Bayleigh appeared from the darkness. But they didn't. Krystal reacted first and did what turned out to be the best thing. She twisted the handlebars and the bike went out from under her.

She hit the road and slid as the bike shot away, drawing sparks from the concrete. He didn't see what happened next because he was already past. And that was when the trap closed. One moment the street was filled with zombies wandering aimlessly. The next they were bearing down on him, arms outstretched to drag him from his bike.

Bayleigh

She heard the bikes and sweat sprung up on her forehead despite the chill air. She had to warn them before they got too close. She dashed from hiding and swore as they appeared in the darkness, headlights like fireflies as they weaved back and forth around the cars. They were going so fast. How were they not hitting anything?

She ran towards them, skirting the trap and into the middle of the road. They saw her but were already too near. One of the bikes went down and slid towards her, throwing sparks into the air. The rider was left behind and swallowed by the darkness. The other bike kept going and drove straight into the trap.

Bayleigh screamed as the zombies closed in. The first, briefly illuminated by the headlamp, was crushed beneath the front wheel. Then hands dragged the rider off and the bike twisted and flipped through the air. She caught a flash of white and a police sign before the bike came thundering down.

Her eyes, though, were already on the rider. It had to be Luke, it was too big to be Krystal. He thrashed around within the circle of zombies but she was already moving, charging towards him. She glanced at the knife in her hand and almost stopped. But before she could, she was there.

The first zombie she reached got the knife in the back of the skull. It dug deep and she heaved. It was like pushing a knife through cooked meat. She yanked it free and leapt over the falling corpse.

The street lights gave just enough for her to see Luke, still with his helmet on, and now on his feet. He'd even drawn his sword, but there was no room to swing it. She gave her full attention to the next zombie. They hadn't spotted her yet and this one she stabbed in the ear. She felt things crack as she drove it home and bile burnt the back of her throat.

Another one down and plenty more to go. The next realised she was there and turned, taking her blade straight through the eye. It was far easier, so long as she didn't look at the ruined eyeball leaking over the blade. Warmth spread down her fingers as the juice from the eyeball spread onto them. She blocked it out, blocked out everything except the next zombie.

This one was ready, its hands outstretched and flailing. And blocking her blow. She hammered at its left arm, digging the blade into the soft flesh until something gave way and the arm dropped useless to its side. The zombie grabbed for her with the other arm but she leant to the side and stabbed it in the cheek.

The blow wasn't clean and went nowhere near its brain. It twisted and the movement nearly yanked the blade from her hand. She clung on and the knife came free. She stabbed again. This time she didn't have the power and it lodged momentarily in the creature's skull. Its clawed hand slammed across the side of her head and she staggered.

Bayleigh's feet caught on the corpse behind her and she fell, landing on something soft. On either side of her, wide-eyed corpses stared, the smell of rot like a shield around them. She couldn't handle this. She kicked out and flailed with her hands, feeling as clumsy as a zombie as her instincts took over. But they were the wrong instincts. She couldn't get out until the creature leaning over her was dead. Its weight landed on her legs. She wasn't going to get out of here.

Something bright struck the zombie just above the ear and the next moment it was missing the top of its head. As loose brain matter trickled down its face, it toppled to one side. Krystal offered her a hand and Bayleigh scrambled to her feet.

'You saved my life.'

'Lots of that going round today. You alright?'

Bayleigh nodded and hefted her knife. 'Is he still alive?'

Krystal didn't answer. She was already wading through the circle of zombies. Only they no longer surrounded Luke. More and more of them were turning to fix their eyes on Krystal. Bayleigh frowned and stared at the girl. One of the zombies moved and for a second Krystal was lit by the street lights. Her left leg was covered in blood, her trouser leg completely torn away.

Bayleigh shook her head, the sweat that covered her going cold. She shivered and leapt forward, driving her knife into the foremost zombie's face. Krystal shouted something and attacked, sword flashing in the night.

Luke joined with them, his own sword covered in blood. The three of them stood in a circle, shoulder to shoulder, and Bayleigh felt like an actor in a movie, the Three Musketeers or something. Then a claw got through and Krystal's face started to bleed. Bayleigh slipped on something and her knee landed so hard she couldn't put weight on it.

'Time's up. Come with me.'

Luke sounded so matter of fact she didn't pause to wonder how he thought they were going any-where. She grabbed his sleeve and he dragged her along. Claws grabbed at her but she ducked and twisted and they fell away. Krystal was right beside her, sword still flicking this way and that. She only took a few steps before she emerged from the crush. Of the zombies that had attacked from the trap, the vast majority were slain, lying in piles on the concrete. Beyond them, the street was peaceful.

They took another few steps before Bayleigh sunk to the ground, followed by Krystal. A number of zombies were still up, but they were digging greedily into the corpses of their pack mates. Bayleigh sat beneath the streetlights and watched a zombie chew the lips off another, then dig its fingers into the half-exposed mouth to pull out the tongue.

All she could think was how glad she was that Layla was properly dead and not out there, doing the same thing. She wouldn't think about Ali at all. She couldn't. Luke hauled her up and pointed at the hospital. With a grunt, she followed him and they staggered through the front doors.

The reception area was littered with dead zombies, but there was no sign of Ed or Alex among them. She was halfway up the stairs when Alex appeared at the top and she staggered, smacking one knee against a step. She heaved herself up and kept going.

He caught her at the top and wrapped his arm around her, helping her stagger down the corridor. She glanced back and saw, as they reached the top of the stairs, Luke scoop Krystal up in his arms and carry her down the corridor. She muttered something, batting at him with arms like a rag doll's, but he ignored her.

They reached the field and stumbled into the private room. Ed waited with bowls of water and cloths and bandages ready. The most surprising thing was that water and cloths was all she needed. She slumped onto one of the beds and watched them examine Krystal. Her leg was a mess, the skin stripped from her slide along the concrete. That the slide had probably saved her life didn't help Bayleigh feel any better.

It was her fault she'd fallen off. If she'd thought of something quicker and reacted better, she could have avoided it.

Alex and Ed set to work on her, clumsily cleaning the wound and binding it in bandage. She didn't know any more than them whether that was the best thing to do, but at this point it was the only thing to do. She peered out of the window. The street looked peaceful. The pile of bodies was attracting more and more zombies, but the slurp and crack of their feasting didn't reach up here.

Some were on all fours, mouths sunk deep into open stomachs or clamped around legs. But others were sat up, holding their chosen arm or foot like chicken legs as they gnawed the meat from the bone. In less than a week they had changed and moved on from the mindless animal behaviour. They weren't human again, not yet, but they no longer moved like beasts. Where would they be in another week, another month?

She turned away from the window and took a deep breath. She should be exhausted, ready to sleep. But her eyes were wide open and refusing to close. She suddenly hated her new-found power. She longed to slip away and lose herself, let the night wash everything away. But she knew that when she did get to sleep it would be for a few hours at best.

Luke sat on the edge of her bed. 'You saved our lives.' He was looking at her differently. She wasn't sure how, but it made her glow and squirm at the same time.

'No I didn't. I hurt Krystal really bad and you'd have got out of there without me.'

He shook his head, smiling wryly. 'No, I don't think so. It's okay to save my life, really. Krystal's already done it today as well. I'm getting quite used to it, if I'm honest.'

She blinked and tried to smile at him. 'Why are you wearing a chef's outfit?'

He glared. 'Long story.'

A little while later they were sat across three beds. Ed was sullen, face hidden by his hair. Alex had told her he'd explain it when he got the chance. He was sitting beside Luke and looked taller than before she went out. He'd killed the zombies in reception, and the blood-soaked baseball bat in the corner was now his weapon of choice. That he had a weapon of choice made her sad, but she was also relieved he could defend himself. The less of them she had to worry about, the better.

Luke was tired and still suffering from his time in the river. He'd given them a rough outline of what happened during their 'routine' scouting trip. It was, he said, a good reminder that nothing was routine in the new world. He was also very pleased at what they'd found in the warehouse.

Krystal was asleep, snoring gently with her head tipped back to face the ceiling. Her leg was a mess but Alex was fairly confident it was nothing permanent. Luke assured them Krystal had earnt at least a week in bed.

The plan had changed a little. They were no longer heading to the country tomorrow. They would rest a few days while they found the right vehicle.

And they would search for Dave and Jackson. Bayleigh had tried to explain the Dave situation in full, with Alex chipping in when she forgot certain things, but Luke still couldn't accept what had happened. She'd only just stopped him from storming into the ladies and giving them a mouthful of abuse.

Luke was confident he wasn't dead. So he could be found. As for Jackson and the other ladies, Luke seemed less bothered about them. He said, with a wry smile on his face, that Jackson was probably doing all he could to keep them safe. They would look for him, but the priority now was to get those that were left out of the city.

But first, a rest. Bayleigh laid her head on the pillow and closed her eyes. Sleep was a long time coming.

Thirteen Roses continues in Book Five: Home

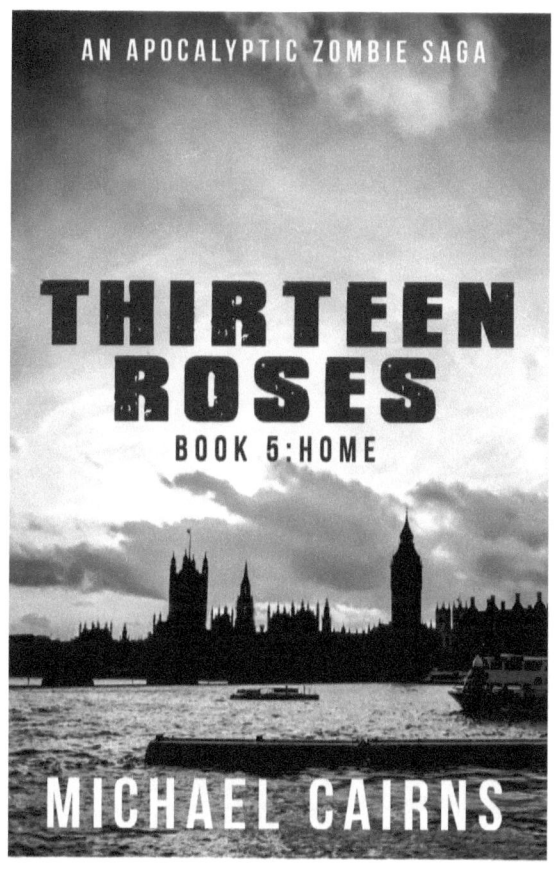

REVIEWS MAKE THE WORLD GO ROUND

Thirteen Roses continues in *Book Four: Alone*.
You can get a digital copy for FREE just by
leaving a review of *Thirteen Roses Book One:
Before* on Amazon, and then telling me about
it.

Email a link to your review to
michael@cairnswrites.com for your free copy!

If you enjoyed what you read, please,
JOIN MY MAILING LIST!

You'll receive a free digital novella of your
choice; regular, exclusive short stories in a
variety of strange and wonderful genres; and
updates on upcoming books. This will include
the chance to get them early at a reduced
price!

cairnswrites.com

Acknowledgements

Thanks to my Mum and Dad. Said it before, I'll probably say it again. They're amazing and are a great part of the reason I'm writing today. They rock.

ABOUT THE AUTHOR

Michael Cairns is a writer and author of a whole bunch of books, involving strange shit happening to strange people, across a wide range of genres. A musician, father and teacher, when not writing he can be found behind his drum kit, tucking into his chocolate stash or trying, and usually failing, to outwit his young daughter.

You can find Michael at:
www.cairnswrites.com
www.twitter.com/cairnswrites
www.facebook.com/cairnswrites
www.goodreads.com/michaelcairns
www.pinterest.com/michaelcairns